THE TICKING CLOCK

Angels & Imperfection Book 3

DAN ARNOLD

The Ticking Clock
by Dan Arnold

Paperback Edition

CKN Christian Publishing
An Imprint of Wolfpack Publishing

6032 Wheat Penny Avenue
Las Vegas, NV 89122

This book is a work of fiction. Any references to historical events, real people or real places are used fictitiously. Other names, characters, places and events are products of the author's imagination, and any resemblance to actual events, places or persons, living or dead, is entirely coincidental.

Paperback ISBN: 978-1-64734-176-3
Ebook ISBN: 978-1-64734-175-6
Library of Congress Control Number: 2020936900

THE TICKING CLOCK

DEDICATION

To Lora
You know what they say,
Third time's a charm,
or three strikes and you're out!
Thank you for believing in me.

To my family, in all its variety and generations
Thank you for challenging me in ways you can't
imagine, encouraging me to keep at it, and being
the wind beneath my wings.

If you read this work, I hope you enjoy it and learn
something about life, yourself, and a little about
the author.

FOREWORD

Since the dawn of time
there's been continuous mortal combat,
both seen and unseen, on earth and in heaven.
It is a struggle for the fate of all created beings.
On earth, predators seek to devour the sheep.
The Shepherds are appointed to stand between the
sheep and the wolves.

PROLOGUE

As he eased along the wall toward the black, cave-like opening of the long-abandoned warehouse, Detective Lieutenant Tony Escalante flicked the safety off his .40 caliber Sig Sauer P226 service weapon.

Where was Tucker?

He had found the man's truck parked at the side of the road.

The moon was the only source of illumination. Tony wasn't sure if he should be pleased or disturbed. The half full orb was scudding in and out of the clouds, providing only dim and intermittent light. The darkness made him all but invisible in the shadows at the edge of the building, but that worked both ways. He was feeling his way along the wall, as much as seeing it.

He was right next to the opening now. He would have to go in — soon. First, his trained eyes scanned the area for any threat or other sign of life. Out in the shifting shadows created by the unreliable moonlight, nothing could be seen moving on the empty plain of oil sand between here and the road, or in the weed choked area beyond. It was as if he were alone in this place.

Wouldn't that be nice?

The last thing in the world he wanted to do was

go into the building. This was typical of the kinds of situations he found himself in, whenever he got a phone call from his friend, J.W.

He knew if things went south, he'd regret not calling for back-up. An unobserved grimace and slight shake of his head were the only indicators as he acknowledged to himself, he wasn't going to make the call.

Drawing a deep breath, he ducked inside. He stayed low and immediately put his back to the inside wall. He was thankful he hadn't tripped over something, slammed into some hidden obstacle or been shot by an unseen assassin. After a moment, he calmed his breathing, and began to listen.

"Hello, detective, I've been expecting you." The voice beside him whispered.

CHAPTER 1

Rosie Ferguson was last seen at her high school, on the day she turned eighteen. Her parents were certain she was with Jimmy Duncan, her former — possibly current, boyfriend. The one who had put her in the hospital a few weeks back.

Jimmy was twenty years old. He grew up in the foster care system and was working at an auto repair shop. Because of what happened to Rosie, he had been arrested on assault charges. Now, he was out on bail. He didn't visit her in the hospital, and as far as her parents knew, he didn't try to see her when she got home. According to the restraining order, he wasn't supposed to get within three hundred feet of Rosie, about the length of a football field.

Then, she disappeared.

Her car was found where she usually parked in the high school lot. She hadn't packed a bag. It was believed she took her purse and her cell phone with her, but she hadn't called or texted anyone.

The police weren't much help. There was only so much they could do. They put out an APB for Duncan's car. It was found in a town about thirty miles away, abandoned. There was no sign of him — or Rosie.

Everyone in the community was trying to help.

There were prayer vigils and active petitioning across every avenue of social media. Posters with their pictures were all-over town and throughout the county.

"Rosie Ferguson is missing! If you see this girl, please call the police. She may be in the company of Jimmy Duncan. If you have any idea where he might be, please call the police. He was last seen in Lindale, Texas. He may be driving a green, 2008 Chevy pickup. If you have any information…"

There were rumors and stories but no one knew anything certain.

After nearly two weeks of heartache and fear, Rosie's parents called me. We arranged to meet in my office.

I'm a private detective.

****

"Mr and Mrs Ferguson, I'll do everything I can, but if the police haven't gotten any leads, I can't make any promises. Are you sure your daughter hasn't been in contact with any of her friends?"

"The police tell us her cell phone hasn't been used since she went missing." Mrs. Ferguson said.

I took a long slow breath.

"As I understand it, the Duncan boy is also missing. He disappeared at the same time Rosie did. Is this the only reason you think she might be with him?"

"They were dating, until…" She couldn't finish the statement.

"Yes, ma'am. Did Rosie give ya'll any reason to believe she was seeing him again, or might run off with Jimmy Duncan?"

Mrs. Ferguson hesitated to speak, then just shook her head, hot tears welling in her eyes. I pushed a box of tissues across the top of my desk toward her.

As she was gathering tissues, Mr. Ferguson said, "We thought she was through with him. This wasn't the first time he had hurt her, but we intended it would be the last. She told us she never wanted to see him again."

I nodded my understanding.

"With the restraining order and him not being a student, if he were seen at the school, you'd think someone would've reported it," I said.

They were both silent.

"What? Did someone report seeing him?"

"No. None of Rosie's friends, or his, will tell us anything. The girls all seem to think Jimmy Duncan is 'dreamy' and together they are a magical couple, like Romeo and Juliet." Mrs. Ferguson said.

"If they won't talk to you, where did you get that idea?"

"Facebook. I've been watching what Rosie's friends have been saying about all this. Everyone thinks they've run off together." She said.

"But you don't."

Mr. Ferguson said, "We think he took her. He lured her into his car, somehow, and drove away with her."

"That might be indicated by the fact she hasn't made any attempt to contact you."

"That's what we're thinking."

"On the other hand, if she did run off with him, she might not want to talk to ya'll about it."

Mr. Ferguson crossed his arms and leaned back in his chair.

"Why would she do something like that?"

"Love, between young girls and bad boys. It happens."

"Not after the way he treated her."

I rubbed my eyelids. How many times had I seen this? Parents wanted to believe the best about their children. Parents want the best for their children and try to lead them in the direction they should go.

Children often want to live their own lives, their

way. Sometimes the two different views can't be reconciled. Once children start approaching adulthood their skills at deception improve exponentially. The things they consider personal and private are often expertly hidden from their parents.

Family dynamics are complex and difficult for outsiders to see or interpret. Appearances can be deceiving. Like a muddy East Texas creek, things are seldom as simple as the surface suggests. Relationships run deep and are often filled with unseen currents, troublesome personalities and unhealthy conditions.

"About that, I know you had Jimmy Duncan arrested for assault. Ya'll pressed charges against him because, at the time, Rosie was still a minor. Were there any witnesses to the assault?"

"No. She was alone with him when it happened. He beat her up because she told him she wanted to break up with him." Mr. Ferguson said. His body language and expression suggested he wasn't interested in discussing the matter further.

Mrs. Ferguson was crying.

"As I said, I'll look into it. The thing is I can't make any promises. I have to look at every possibility and follow every lead. I don't know where that will take me, or what I'll discover. Are y'all prepared for the outcome, no matter which way it goes?"

Mrs. Ferguson clutched the tissue, now balled up in her white knuckled fist.

"Do you think he may have…?"

"No, Ma'am. I'm not speculating about anything. All I'm saying is we don't know all the facts yet. Ya'll may not like everything I learn. This situation could go a very different direction than we expect."

Mrs. Ferguson gave her husband a worried look.

"How soon can you start?" He asked.

"Well, sir, as it happens, I've already started"

****

Mrs. Ferguson supplied me with a list of Rosie's friends. I researched them on social media, noting the comments and attitudes they were so willing to share with the world, but might not dare to discuss in person. It was just as she had told me. All of Rosie's friends and classmates thought she and Jimmy belonged together. They were viewed as star crossed lovers on the run, part Bonnie and Clyde, part Romeo and Juliet. There was some discussion about whether Jimmy had, or ever could, hurt Rosie.

I was able to persuade Priscilla Davidson, Rosie's best friend, to agree to an interview. I told her I was a PI hired by Rosie's mom. She had heard about me on the news, back when I helped find some missing kids. She would only talk to me if her parents and Rosie's mother were present for the interview. Not Rosie's parents, just Rosie's mom.

When I explained this to Mrs. Ferguson, she was reluctant and sounded like she was afraid to talk with Priscilla. It took considerable coaxing and promises that her husband, Bob, wouldn't know about the meeting, but she eventually succumbed to my silver-tongued charm.

Since Bob Ferguson always played golf on Saturday, we met on Saturday morning at the home of Nancy and Ted Davidson, Priscilla's parents. They were friendly and supportive of Mrs. Ferguson, telling us they had just learned their daughter had been in contact with Rosie.

Priscilla looked like she wanted to run away. She made a face and turned to Mrs. Ferguson.

"… So anyway, Rosie just wants you to know she's safe and happy or whatever."

"Priscilla, how long have you been in contact with Rosie? The police said her cell phone hasn't been used." Mrs. Ferguson asked.

"Jimmy bought one of those pay as you go phones. We mostly just text. They found a safe place to camp and plan to move on as soon as the hub bub dies down."

"But, I'm her mother. Why hasn't she called me?"

"Don't you know why?"

Mrs. Ferguson looked away, a forlorn yet distant expression on her face. She looked as if she would never smile again.

"Do you know where they are?" I asked.

Priscilla looked down at her phone and said, "No. I think it's somewhere in the area, but I don't really know where."

"When you say 'in the area', what gives you that idea? Do you think they're close by?"

"Oh, uhh, no, I don't know, really. I guess I just assumed they were around here somewhere."

I wasn't buying it, but trying to confront her under the present circumstances wouldn't accomplish anything.

I knew Priscilla Davidson worked after school at a local daycare. I planned to stop by and ask her a few more pointed questions, in a time and place where she might feel a bit more vulnerable.

It would have to wait till Monday. That afternoon, I had a funeral to attend.

CHAPTER 2

I arrived at the third-floor office of what I liked to call "the international headquarters" of Tucker Investigations just before eight o'clock on Monday morning. This four-room office was a huge improvement over the single, dingy room in a strip mall I had been using just a year or so before. This newer space, in a bank building right on the south loop, had been used by the ATF before we became the tenants. When the feds moved out, they left the bulletproof walls and windows in place, as well as the keypad locks on the doors. I had had new security cameras mounted to the housings they had left behind.

Inside, the walls were all paneled in oak, including my corner office with windows that looked out over the forested city below. My associate, Christine Valakova had carefully chosen the furniture and appointments, giving this space the appearance of an upscale agency. Even my heavily carved oak desk, with the two upholstered wingback chairs in front, was there due to her efforts. I had been using a folding plastic table from Walmart when she first came into my life.

Seated behind her desk in the reception area, Christine greeted me with a tenuous smile. She wore a black suit with a knee length skirt and what might've been a man's open neck, white dress shirt. The black and white made her radiant red hair appear even more stunning. For me, the black suit was a reminder of the funeral we had attended the day before and perhaps a testimony to her frame of mind.

Today, her jewelry of choice was a small gold cross.

"John, a lady is coming to discuss whether we might be able to help her with a family matter. I didn't know if you would be here. So, I told her I would meet with her. If you would rather do it yourself..."

"Who is she?"

"Her name is Hafsah Mohammad. How's that for a, a Muslim name?"

"Egyptian, I think. I believe her name means 'married to the prophet'. I wonder if she's related to Izzy?"

"Who is Izzy?"

"Issa Mohammad. He goes by Izzy. He has a pretty successful investment and insurance business here in town."

"It seems likely doesn't it? How many people named Mohammad would live in little old Tyler, Texas?"

"I have no idea. Probably more than we might expect. The name is popular and considered a great honor in the Muslim world. In this country, the name is fashionable with prison inmates, others who convert to Islam and the proponents of the Nation of Islam."

"Is that another name for ISIS or the Islamic State?"

"No, it's an American racist group that espouses quasi Muslim ideals. Is Ms. Mohammad a lady of color?"

"I don't know. She has a barely discernible foreign accent; it's more refined than East Texas, maybe even more British than American."

"Hmmm, did she say what she wanted to talk about?"

"No, just that it's a private family matter."

"I think it might be best for you to meet with

her. If she observes the cultural restraints of some of the Islamic countries, she would probably be more comfortable talking to you."

"OK, I'll do it. She'll be here in about ten minutes."

On my monitor, a few minutes later, I watched Ms. Mohammad come into our outer office to be greeted by Christine. The lady was a knockout, and not at all what I had been expecting.

That was odd. What was I expecting?

A moment later Christine came in, closing the door behind her.

"John, she wants to confer with you."

"And it's a problem because...?"

"When she called to set up the appointment, I told her I didn't think you would be in the office at all today. Now, somehow she knows you're here."

I smiled.

"Does that seem funny to you?" Christine asked.

"Uh huh, it's funny odd, not funny laughable. Does she want to meet with both of us, or just me?"

"With just you. Apparently, I'm not to be included."

"Interesting..."

"I'll say. So much for 'cultural restraints'. Not to mention how she knows you're here. Shall I send her in?"

"No, please bring her in and introduce us."

Christine smiled at me.

"You saw her on the monitor, didn't you?"

A moment later, she ushered Ms. Mohammad into my office. I stood up to greet them as they came in.

"John, this is Hafsah Mohammad. Ms. Moham-mad, may I present John Wesley Tucker?"

I love it when Christine gets all formal and what not.

Ms. Mohammad was about five feet nine inches tall in her high heels, slim and very well dressed. Her sleeveless dress was closely tailored and appeared to be some sort of textured silk in a color I could only call "peacock" blue. Dark hair fell in cascading swirls to her shoulders. Her complexion was much darker than Christine's, what we would call olive, I suppose. It was warm and natural. No darker a shade than most high school cheerleaders achieved after baking for hours in tanning beds. Her makeup was flawless, and it was difficult to determine her age. Her dark, almond shaped eyes locked onto mine.

Momentarily stunned, I couldn't look away.

"I'm very pleased to meet you, Mr. Tucker," she said, as she extended her hand across the desk. "I appreciate you taking the time to meet with me."

"My pleasure, Ms. Mohammad, please have a seat. May I offer you coffee or tea?"

"No, thank you, and please call me Hafsah. May I call you John?" She asked, as she selected a chair.

"John, if you'll excuse me, I have a matter requiring my immediate attention," Christine said.

"OK, say hello to Tony for me." I replied, sitting down myself. I figured Christine was going to call her boyfriend, Tony Escalante. Tony is also my best friend and the detective Lieutenant in the Robbery Homicide Division of the Tyler PD.

As Christine left the room, she glanced over to Ms. Mohammad and made a face at me. I wasn't sure how to interpret her expression.

Women. Go figure.

I studied Ms. Mohammad for a moment. I liked everything I saw. Her appearance, her poise and even the sound of her voice were appealing. That was all well and good, but there was something about her which I found disquieting. Something she had awakened in me. What was it about her that had such a strong, nearly staggering effect on me?

"Forgive my asking, Ms. Mohammad, where are you from?"

"I take it you have observed I am not from here, John. Please call me, Hafsah. Where do you think I might be from?"

"Your clothing is expensive and rather European, designer?"

She smiled. "The dress and shoes are Soporo of Paris. You really are perceptive."

"Maybe, but you are not from France."

"Pourquoi dites-vous cela?"

"Because of your speech pattern, I'd say you were born in the Middle East, and learned to speak both French and English there."

She raised her delicate eyebrows.

"Full marks, John."

"You're Lebanese, I think, although your name is Egyptian."

She shrugged. "My mother was Lebanese. I am a woman of the world."

"Should we talk about your father?"

She scowled at me.

"No. I did not come here for that."

I studied her some more. I found the process… enjoyable. She became aware of my gaze and, perhaps made uncomfortable by it, shifted in the upholstered armchair. My embarrassment brought me back to my senses.

"How can we be of assistance?"

"I am looking for a relative. I have reason to believe he has come here, to Tyler. Perhaps you can help me find him?"

"A relative…?"

"Yes, he is my cousin, actually. His name is Nazim."

"Nazim Mohammad?"

She shook her head.

"His name is Nazim Bahadur. He is here on business. We have not heard from him since his arrival. As you will understand, we have some concern for his… well-being."

I observed her body language and decided she was guarded. She was only telling me part of the story.

"When did he arrive?"

"Perhaps within the last week, give or take a few days."

"… Perhaps? You don't know when he arrived? How did he get here? If he traveled by plane I'd think you'd know his itinerary."

"This is why I am seeking your assistance, John. My cousin Nazim is a musician and something of a free spirit. He hatched this silly plan to pass himself off as a Mexican immigrant. His physical appearance supports the ruse, and recently he spent some time in Spain where he learned to speak acceptable Spanish. A few weeks ago, he flew into Mexico and we believe, shortly later he crossed the border with a hired guide."

"Coyote," I said.

"Pardon me?"

"They're called coyotes. The hired guide you referred to."

"Ah yes, so they are. My cousin is probably calling himself, Nat Baha. It is a stage name, the name he performs under as a musician."

"Let me see if I understand what you just told me. You say your cousin, a man named Nazim Bahadur, came into the US by sneaking across the border from Mexico. He's pretending to be someone named Nat Baha. He presumably came to Tyler, but you don't know exactly when he got here, or where he is now. Is that about right?"

"To sum it up, yes, those are the pertinent details. Do you think you can help me ascertain his whereabouts?"

Talk about a tall tale! This nearly took the cake. Why in the world would someone go to such elaborate risks just to come to Texas?

"Maybe you should go to the police." I suggested.

"That would seem logical, but it would not be my first choice. You do understand he is here in your country illegally? Given the concerns about certain people from the Middle East sneaking into America by crossing the border with Mexico, I can hardly go to the authorities." She looked deeply into my eyes.

I was lost for a moment. The connection really was staggering. Something like an electric current swept through me. My past and future whirled around and seemed to re-align. This had never happened before. There was something at work here beyond my understanding. I've learned to guard my heart. My normal modus operandi is to remain aloof, maintaining a professional distance. In her eyes I found something that shook the foundation of my self-built isolation.

"How is it you haven't heard from him for so long?" I managed.

She closed her eyes and broke the connection. Pausing for a moment, she blinked and swallowed, as though somewhat shaken herself. She recovered quickly, clearing her throat.

"As I said, he is a free spirit. At times, he can be rather... unpredictable. This is all a lark to him."

"You say he's here on business. Does he have business contacts here?"

"I believe so. He is supposed to be visiting someone in the music business. Someone who can help him get a recording made, but there is a family matter requiring his immediate attention. So, I must find him as quickly as possible."

"What sort of family matter?" I asked.

She stiffened a bit, as though offended by the question, "A death in the family, John, I'm sure you understand."

Alarm bells were ringing in my head. Had she just told me more than she intended? No, I was pretty sure she had phrased her response with precision. If I understood her implied intentions, why had she been sent to me?

Nodding slowly, I said, "Yes, Hafsah, I think I'm beginning to."

After I escorted her out to handle the business arrangements with Christine, I returned to my office and considered the implications of what she had told me.

Something about her story didn't pass the sniff test. More disturbing was the effect she had on me. In her presence I had become somehow vulnerable to feelings and sensations I had long since learned to ignore. How had she slipped past my defenses? The phenomenon had hit me like a bolt of lightning. Did she know what she was doing? Could it be some form of deliberate ploy, or was I experiencing a weird reaction to something about her, like an allergy? No matter how I looked at it, one thing was very clear.

This case would be interesting on several levels.

CHAPTER 3

Waiting for the elevator, Hafsah turned and looked back up the hallway to the office she had just exited. As directed, she had set out to hire a local private investigator to help her make connections in the small Muslim community in this East Texas town. The interview hadn't gone as expected. Although she was thoroughly familiar with the colorful, if somewhat strange facts, outlined in the dossier provided. Even after being generally briefed about the man. For all her information and preparation, she had still been caught completely off guard.

Hafsah Mohammad thought of herself as a professional businesswoman. She managed companies staffed with executives she herself hired. Dealing with capable and strong men in high profile positions was a routine part of both her business and personal life. She was used to establishing agendas and achieving objectives. She was adept at maintaining professional distance and reading the men with whom she did business. Hafsah knew when to be assertive and when to be coy. Her skill set included the full complement of feminine charms, coupled with a laser like focus on achieving a specific outcome. Hiring a small-town PI should've been virtually beneath her. What had just happened?

From the moment she met John Wesley Tucker, she

had been swimming in deep waters. She had intended to inform the man of her requirements, determine the schedule of services provided, and settle the fee structure. At first glance the man appeared athletic, but otherwise ordinary. She worked with men like him all the time. But, when she made eye contact with him, the connection had been nearly overwhelming. It was as if he was looking into her soul, seeing her, the whole her — completely open and unprotected, and for her part — she welcomed it!

In his eyes she saw a depth and intelligence beyond any she had ever seen. More than that, there was so much kindness, acceptance and compassion mixed with some sort of sorrow in his gaze, she found herself almost irresistibly drawn to him. It took all her professional training and commitment to the mission to keep herself on course. Even so, she had lost control of the conversation. The next thing she knew, she was standing out here in the hallway!

The ding of the arriving elevator was like the sound of the bell at the start of another round in a boxing match. It cleared her head and got her back in the fight.

Maybe she was just hormonal. Whatever, she had things to do. She had to find her recalcitrant quarry and she had to find him fast. For the last three months she had been searching, picking up his trail only to find he had already moved on. She nearly caught up with him in Spain, but he slipped away. Now she was two weeks behind him. It was time to stop following him and get out ahead of him.

John Wesley Tucker was just another tool in her toolbox. Either he would help her achieve her goal, or be discarded in favor of someone more capable.

It was strange. As she left the building, she experienced the oddest sensation. It was almost as though she wanted to turn around and go back up to the man's office. It was as if she felt diminished or somehow less herself, the farther she moved away from him.

What was happening to her?

CHAPTER 4

When Priscilla Davidson came out of the daycare building, a little after five that evening, she found me leaning on her car door.

She slowed as she recognized me, stopping several feet away.

I flashed what I hoped was my least threatening and most charming smile.

"Hi, Priscilla, I'm John Wesley Tucker. You remember me, right?"

"Sure, you're the private eye. What do you want?"

"I was wondering if you've talked to Rosie, maybe today."

"Maybe."

"Un uh. Try again. Did you talk to Rosie today?"

"Yeah, so?"

"So, that's a good thing. It seems you're the only person she communicates with. We need you to keep us in the loop."

"Us, who?"

"Her mother and me, of course."

"Have her mother call me. I need to get going." She started toward me like she meant to push me out of the way.

"Is Rosie safe?"

That stopped her. Her mouth firmed into a thin

line, her eyes flashing cold fire.

"Safer than at home."

I nodded and uncrossed my arms, still leaning on her driver's side door.

"I was afraid it might be something like that."

"Like what? You don't know anything."

"Enlighten me."

It was Priscilla's turn to cross her arms, wrapping them around her purse. Her body language telling me she was insecure and defensive.

"Let's just say there's a reason she ran away with Jimmy."

"OK, let's just say there is. Go ahead and tell me why."

"Can't"?

"Can't or won't?"

She shrugged.

"Whatever. Are you going to let me go?"

I nodded and stood up.

"Yes, but I want you to know I'm only trying to help. Your secret is safe with me."

"That's what I told Rosie."

"You've been a good friend to her. I'm a friend as well. If there's anything I can do to help you, Rosie or Jimmy, I will."

I handed her one of my cards. The real one with my business name on it. "Give them my number and tell them to call me at any time if they need to talk to someone. Especially, if they're in danger."

Priscilla looked at my card then back up at me.

"How do I know you won't go telling Mr. Ferguson where they are?"

I winked at her.

"Because I don't know where they are. You and I both know that won't last much longer. I'll tell Mrs. Ferguson they're both safe, for now. Goodbye, Priscilla."

I started to walk away.

"What about Mr. Ferguson?"

I looked back over my shoulder. "What about him?"

Priscilla just shook her head as she unlocked her car door and ducked inside.

As she drove away, I wondered if I should've stood my ground and dug a little deeper. When I gave her my card and told her to give it to Rosie and Jimmy, she forgot she was supposed to tell me she didn't know where they were. I now knew, sure as shooting, she would be paying them a visit.

CHAPTER 5

I was sitting in my living room watching a discussion on CNN. The program was about America in the 21st century. There were four people on the panel, each a well-known commentator on politics and social issues.

There was a knock on my door, so I turned the TV off. I didn't need to hear the four commentator's opinions. There is no end of opinions. Americans tend to be myopic. In the context of the light revealed in ancient scriptures, where do human beings on this planet see the condition of the world at this point in their limited understanding of time? Now that would be a discussion worth watching, but we'll never see it on a major news network. The subject would probably be treated as amusing entertainment on the History Channel, Discovery or even the Comedy Channel.

I found Department of Homeland Security agent Jack McCarthy waiting on the landing outside my door. This wasn't a surprise visit, I had been expecting him. I wasn't expecting him to come in disguise.

"Is it clean?" He asked.

I knew he wasn't referring to my standard of domestic sanitation. He wanted to know if my apartment was free of electronic listening devices or hidden cameras.

Jack is paranoid like that.

I nodded, but turned the TV back on, anyway. The noise would prevent anyone from being able to monitor our conversation from outside the apartment.

"That's some get-up," I said. "It's not Halloween yet. Are you trick or treating?"

Jack now sported a bushy mustache and he had gained about forty-five pounds since I had seen him earlier in the day. I knew the glasses he wore were not prescription. He was carrying a stuffed paper grocery bag from a Brookshire's supermarket.

Jack shrugged and said, "Better safe than sorry."

"Is all this cloak and dagger stuff really necessary?"

"I don't know who might be watching your apartment."

"Oh come on, really?"

He made a face. "Wait till you hear what I have to tell you."

"Well then, let's get to it."

We both took seats on the antique sofa, still upholstered in the original speckled cowhide from when I had first acquired it. Jack pulled photos and documents out of the grocery bag, spreading them out on the old steamer trunk I used as a coffee table. He got straight to the point.

"You were right. Her name isn't 'Hafsah Mohammad'. It's Hafsah Bashir."

We were looking at a still photo taken from the video my office security cameras had recorded earlier in the day. There were several other pictures.

"Her mother was Lebanese and her father Egyptian. Long story short, we're pretty sure she's an Israeli intelligence asset. We believe she works for Mossad."

"Yeah, I figured it was something like that."

"We knew she was here in the U.S. She flew into L.A. six days ago. Then she disappeared."

"Mighty easy for people to disappear, even with you Homeland Security types watching, isn't it?"

"She's a pro, John. She has contacts and resources

all over the world. DHS has to watch a lot of people."

"I understand. I'm just rattling your cage."

"This guy," Jack said, tapping another photo, "is Nazim Bahadur, a/k/a Hakim Muktallah. This is the most recent photo we have, and it's a couple of years old. Born Saudi, but he has several passports and claims Islam as his only nationality. He's a bad, bad boy who dropped off the radar about six weeks ago. He was on the active radar because he's probably responsible for a number of killings of Israelis and others, in various locations around the world. Muktallah is the prime suspect in that murder in Barcelona where several people, including the French Ambassador's wife and child, were machine gunned to death. It wasn't called 'terrorism' at the time, because it was thought he was just one man acting alone. A couple of days later, the Caliphate claimed responsibility for it. By then, he had already disappeared from Europe. He's like a damned magician, the way he vanishes. In whatever way he got into Mexico we missed him. He must've been using a new alias. I don't have to tell you what all this means."

"Hafsah said he uses the name Nat Baha. Probably has a passport in that name."

"Could be, it would explain why he was able to escape Europe and why we missed him in Mexico. We'll add that name to the list."

"Where was this Mr. Baha trained?" I asked.

"His past is sketchy. We believe when he was still just a teenager, he left Saudi Arabia to fight with the Taliban in Afghanistan and Pakistan. Since then, he's been in Lebanon, Syria, Iraq, Yemen, even Sudan. He's trained ISIL fighters and members of Hezbollah. Over the last two years or so, he's traveled the world killing enemies of Islam. He's been everywhere."

"How is he funded?"

"His family is wealthy, but our sources say they've

cut their ties with him. He's probably burned through whatever money he had. We believe the Islamic State is funding his missions"

"Do you think he's really here, now?"

"What do you think?"

"I think there would be no reason for Mossad to send an agent into East Texas, without alerting our intelligence people, if he weren't here."

"There's something else you should know."

"And that is?"

"He really is Hafsah Bashir's cousin."

CHAPTER 6

Jack's news was troubling. DHS had sent him here because of a suspected threat from a self-radicalized jihadist cell. Now Mossad had sent an agent to track down a known terrorist. That agent was disturbing me in ways I didn't yet understand. I couldn't help thinking about the old adage, "trouble always comes in threes." While it wasn't what I wanted to hear, it didn't come as a complete surprise. It did raise some questions.

"Why would a Mossad agent come to me? I'm just a private investigator in East Texas. This Muktallah cat is an international terrorist. Why wouldn't they alert the CIA and the FBI to help track this guy down?"

"Mossad conducts the international intelligence operations for the nation of Israel. As you know, they have another agency similar to our FBI, called Shin Bet. They handle most of the internal intelligence operations for Israel. Shin Bet will often interface with the FBI.

Mossad is a different story. They like to handle Israel's foreign intelligence ops themselves and they don't always play well with others. There are many reasons they don't like to work with the CIA or the FBI. For example, Mossad operates with far fewer layers of bureaucracy and less accountability than any of our federal agencies, which are all interconnected on some level. With so many different agencies, committees and people involved, we have a serious problem keeping anything secret. Look at what Ed Snowden was able to do. Knowing this, our Israeli friends like to play their cards close to the vest."

"Come on, you're suggesting Mossad is running a clandestine op on U.S. soil. If that gets out, there will be no end to the stink."

Jack nodded.

"My point. That's the reason they didn't alert the CIA."

"Do I need to remind you that you work for Uncle Sam? Isn't this the kind of thing DHS does, coordinating all the agencies involved in protecting America?"

"No, you don't need to remind me. Let's just say DHS has several different functions. Not all of them are known to the general public. As for informing other agencies, I have some liberty with my discretionary powers. In my judgment, at this point we need to tread lightly, the fewer people who know about this, the better. At the same time, Mossad sending a single agent, and her contacting you, worries me a little. It makes me wonder if she somehow knew you had a connection with me."

"I don't see how. I haven't had any connection with you for several years. You weren't even here a month ago. You just came here to coordinate with the FBI on the white supremacist operation that got my friend killed."

The muscles along Jack's jawline bunched. It was the only indication he was annoyed by my remark.

"I think we need to keep it that way. She doesn't need to know you're working with DHS and the FBI."

"Just to be clear, I'm not working with the FBI. Not after what they did at that farmhouse. And I haven't forgotten your part in it. So, I'm not working with you, either. I only contacted you because you had already given me a heads up about a possible jihadist threat."

"Easy does it, stud. I had no direct involvement in that FBI raid. Whatever happened had nothing to do with me."

"You must have had prior knowledge!"

"We talked about this, John. The whole thing was orchestrated by SAIC Doug Booker. He has political connections, and he was playing a game none of us could imagine. Try to move on."

I considered my options. I could live with it for a little while, at least until I knew what Hafsah's game was, and Jack's.

"We'll see. What do you have in mind?" I asked.

"This Nat Baha character means to kill innocent civilians — as many as he can. Hafsah Bashir was sent here to stop him. She came to you. Can you and I work together or not?"

I crossed my arms, taking a moment to frame my answer.

"I don't like it, but I'll give it a try. Just you, Jack, I'll only work with you. I have no interest in getting back in service with Uncle Sam. Don't send anyone to me in your name, or expect me to report to anyone but you."

"OK, fair enough."

"I'm still wondering why Hafsah Bashir came to me." I said.

"Well, if I was looking for someone in this area to do what she's asking you to do, you would be my first choice. You're known to be a trustworthy and efficient private investigator. She has no contacts in East Texas. It makes sense for her to get with somebody familiar with the locals and has the right connections. Besides, Mossad probably chose you, not Hafsah personally. They would've supplied her with some background on you. She may know more about you than you can imagine."

"How would Mossad know anything about me?"

"How do you think?"

I held my hands up in acquiescence. After all,

there was some history there.

"There's something strange about this, though." I said. "What is it?"

"She practically told me who she is. The false last name 'Mohammad', letting me know there was an Islamic connection. Hafsah admitted her mother was Lebanese. She told me Muktallah had been in Spain recently, and then she tried to feed me that lame story about him being a musician, now known as Nat Baha, looking for a recording contract. I had concluded she wasn't some relative seeking a missing family member. She even hinted she was hunting Baha to kill him."

"That's why you sent me her picture."

"I'm guessing you've already got the CIA involved on this thing, probably NSA too, right?"

"No. You leave that to me. This is my op. I'll inform Langley and the others of this particular wrinkle, if and when I think the time is right."

"Come on, Jack, there's a foreign terrorist right here in East Texas. He came here for a reason. There's an obvious connection to the case you're working."

"Yes, we knew about the local jihadist cell. We've been watching them for a while. After the poorly planned attempts others have made, our analysts suggested there might be some sort of leader coming to train and organize them. We thought we would pick up some electronic traffic that would alert us. None of us anticipated a foreign trainer would just sneak across the border and show up here."

"This guy isn't just a trainer, Jack. He's a killer."

"That's why Ms. Bashir is an asset. She knows him, how he thinks and operates. She has experience dealing with people like him. This is what Mossad does best. We need her and we don't need any interference from some federal oversight committee, or to find ourselves detoured and bogged down by a multi-agency power struggle."

"You must've left a digital trail researching Hafsah and her cousin. You've raised a red flag somewhere. Somebody will be asking you some hard questions. I don't see how you're going to avoid it."

"That's my problem, John. Do you want to see FBI Special Agent, Doug Booker involved in this?"

"No. It would be best if I don't ever see him again."

"We're agreed then. We'll keep a lid on this as long as we can. I'll look into the weapons angle. They'll need to acquire fully automatic weapons, and probably some type of explosives, if they don't already have them."

"Jack, you said you've been watching these people for quite a while, you would know if they were getting explosives and weapons."

"You would think so wouldn't you?"

He began putting the photos and files back into the grocery bag, which he then folded into a thin flat package. When he had tucked it into his waistband along with the other padding under his shirt, he stood up and turned toward the door.

"You can keep the loaf of bread and the celery, compliments of Uncle Sam."

"Gee, thanks. Is that it then, you're leaving?"

"That's all I have for you."

"What am supposed to do? Where do we go from here?" I asked.

Jack turned and looked me in the eye.

"Ms. Bashir hired you to help her find a terrorist in our midst. That man intends to commit an act of horrible evil. You can help her, John. You can do that. Find this guy and stop him."

After Jack left, I took a moment to reflect on the situation. I knew he had lied to me at least once. Jack was fully aware of all the players. He had been sent to East Texas because DHS was monitoring the threat. Someone in his agency, ATF, FBI, NSA or all the above, had kept the local suspects under close scrutiny for some time. Jack knew the weapons had already been procured. If he had people watching the suspects, he probably would have people watching me. Jack was keeping things from me, in his mind because of the "need to know" policy in matters of national security. To Jack, I was just a pawn in the game. Jack planned to use me as the go-between with Hafsah, and through her, with Mossad. It wasn't his fault. He was answerable to a higher authority. I had to wonder who was above him pulling the strings.

That thought made me smile. I knew whoever Jack thought was his boss, was someone whose pay grade was still far below my boss.

I had to consider my next move in light of my mission on this planet. I try to avoid involvement in the never-ending power struggles and political machinations of men. I seek the lost sheep and assist those in peril. I stand between the sheep and the wolves and help maintain the course of events in the timeline established by my King.

On occasion the wolves have pulled me away from my primary mission. I've found myself chasing wolves, instead of seeing to the needs of those sheep assigned to me. Was this one of those situations? Was this an attempt to lead me away from my mission? I needed to be alert and aware of all the possible pitfalls and snares.

I knew the Department of Homeland Security, through Jack McCarthy, was using me and keeping secrets. There were several things Jack wasn't telling me. Hafsah was probably doing the same thing, but for different reasons.

The Mossad agent faced great peril in service to others, but her struggle was in matters of the world. My response to her was on some level a matter of the flesh. That temptation is ever with us Shepherds as we travel through this life in our "earth suits"

Did Hafsah's mission coincide with my mission, or did her presence conflict with my mission? Every person serves in the purpose of someone. Bob Dylan said it best. "Well, it might be the devil, or it might be the Lord, but you gotta serve somebody."

Who did Hafsah serve? Should I stand aside and watch events unfold?

And there it was. Hafsah was willing to sacrifice herself to defend people she had never met. Her cousin Bahadur was a predator, determined to attack the helpless. He and the pack of wolves he was forming would stop at nothing in the process of destroying others. If I merely observed, I would neglect a duty and an opportunity.

I saw it as my duty to help Hafsah in her hunt for Bashir. My mission required me to help her defend the helpless. To do less in the time I have left, would be wrong.

CHAPTER 7

Walking through the throngs of people in the indoor shopping mall, Hakim was almost dancing, he felt so energized and powerful. For all the sublime celestial juice flowing through him, no one noticed him. He was just another face in the crowd, part of the everyday life of the local citizens. These silly sheep had no idea he was a vicious predator disguised in sheep's clothing. He had entered their country illegally, he was carrying an unauthorized weapon, and he intended to commit mass murder. Yet, to these sheep he was invisible. It was but one of his gifts. He was like a chameleon, blending in with the local environment, unnoticed until he struck. Soon now, he would strike in this place.

His life's work had been revealed to him in a vision given by Allah. Had not Allah sent his own heavenly messenger? In all his travels and travails, had he not been led to victory by this angel? Whatever limited direction he had been given by the leaders of the Caliphate was as nothing compared to that of his guiding angel. Allah had gifted him in several other extraordinary ways.

For as long as he could remember he had played guitar. Wherever he traveled, the popular western music was blasting from some sort of speaker.

Today, after more than thirty years of practice, he could play as well as, or better than, anyone he had ever heard.

For all his love of western music, he hated with an equal passion, anyone who interfered in the affairs of the people of Islam. This was far too common with the westerners, the European and American infidels in particular. He was a teenager when Osama Bin Laden sent several of his own countrymen to attack America by flying airplanes into their symbols of power. He left Saudi Arabia to join the cause of jihad in Afghanistan as a foot soldier of Bin Laden. His nimble fingers now learned how to tear the life away from his fellow human beings. Adept at hand-to-hand combat, he became skilled with knives, handguns, machineguns and rifles. He learned to make explosives and detonators from compounds and common materials found available anywhere in the world. His skills were in demand throughout the region. In a time when young men his age were blowing themselves up in the process of killing their enemies, he was building the bombs.

At first, he was available to whoever would pay him, Sunni or Shiite. Killing each other as often as not. He began to train those less skilled than himself. At various training camps he honed his personal fighting skills. He found his true calling — murdering the unsuspecting. For a time, he had wondered if he might be mad, but the angel of Allah changed his thinking. His angel led him to people and places where his knowledge and skills were in demand. He began killing Jews and high-profile infidels all around the globe. In all that time, wherever he went and whoever he killed, in the company of the angel he slipped away unmolested. He was that cunning. He felt the constant presence of the angel, leading and directing him, telling him there was a still higher purpose for his life.

His successful carnage had attracted the attention

of various police and intelligence agencies. They were determined to capture or kill him. He learned that more than one of the Middle Eastern agencies, for whom he had done wet work, had betrayed him for little more than political expediency. He had always been expendable and now he was considered more of a liability than an asset.

In the aftermath of the American's war against Iraq, following the Arab Spring and the civil war in Syria, the Islamic State in Iraq and Syria had sprung up like a mushroom. The leadership of ISIS saw him as an instrument designed for their particular purpose. He was nothing less than the personification of their ideals. They took him in like a long-lost son. At first, because of his experience and language skills, he was tasked with training the recruits from western countries. When his trainees proved to be deadlier than the local boys, he was offered elevation to command status. Because he preferred to do things his own way, he'd never been comfortable in any military unit. He had always hated being in uniform. He asked to be sent overseas to conduct foreign operations for the Islamic State. His request was granted. It served the goals in the Daesh mission statement. Like him, it was their plan to see Islam conquer the world in the name of Allah. This would be accomplished by reclaiming any lands that had once been part of Islam, any lands where a mosque or mosques now stood and eventually all other lands.

Most of the western nations were ripe for the plucking.

Recruiting disenfranchised young people in these countries through the internet was effective, but they lacked the requisite skillset and often failed to accomplish any meaningful mission. They needed leadership and training. This was work he could do with extraordinary ability. His handlers at the command level secured funding for each operation and provided him with logistical support. Beyond that, they left him to select specific targets and work out the details on his own. His mission in Spain had been a huge success, but although ISIL claimed responsibility for the attack, in the intelligence community all eyes were on him. His handlers in the Islamic State arranged for him to escape Europe and instructed him to make his way to a group of eager self-proclaimed recruits in Texas, USA. His mission was to train them as mujahedeen, holy warriors of jihad.

Now, he believed everything he had ever done, all the hard work and personal sacrifice would culminate in his greatest triumph. Here, in this place, he would fulfill his destiny.

CHAPTER 8

As if my day hadn't been long and strange enough already, my phone started ringing the moment Jack walked out the door.

"Good evening, John Tucker, here. How can I help you?"

"Mr. Tucker? This is Priscilla Davidson, Rosie's friend. Do you remember me?"

"Of course, Priscilla, how are you?"

"I'm worried. Rosie hasn't texted me since last night."

"It's probably nothing to worry about. Maybe her phone is dead, or they've used up all the time and data they paid for. You told me it was a pre-paid phone, right?"

"Right, but she would've told me if they needed money or something."

"OK, so it's probably just a dead battery."

"They have a phone charger in the truck."

That was interesting and useful information. There had been some speculation about Rosie and Jimmy having been seen in a green Chevy pickup, but no real proof. Not only was Priscilla confirming the vehicle was a truck, she knew they had a phone charger in it.

"Did she tell you that?"

"Umm, yeah. I know they have plenty of gas, so they should be able to keep the phone charged."

Now, Priscilla was telling me both too much and too little. How could she know how much fuel they had in the pickup?

"Have you been giving them money, Priscilla?"

"That doesn't matter. I'm afraid something happened to them." She was almost wailing now.

"Calm down. Just because she hasn't texted you today doesn't mean something bad happened. Maybe they're traveling or there's something wrong with the phone."

"No. I've sent her like twenty texts and she never got back to me."

"Again, that's no reason to jump to conclusions. Give her some time. She'll probably contact you in a day or two."

"Mr. Tucker, the truck is still there."

"Still where, are you saying you've seen it? You know where they are?"

"I probably shouldn't tell you... You've got to promise not to tell anyone, if I tell you."

"OK. Let's take a moment to think about this. I need to ask you some questions. Can I do that?"

"I guess. It depends on what you want to know."

"How long have you known where they are?"

"... Pretty much since they ran off together."

"Why did they run off?"

"I can't tell you that."

I took a deep breath and let it out slowly, gathering my thoughts.

"Have you seen them since they disappeared?"

Priscilla hesitated before she answered.

"Yes."

"Where are they?"

"I don't know, that's why I called you."

"You said you know where the truck is. You said, 'It's still there'. Where is it, Priscilla?"

"Do you know where the old abandoned warehouse is on County Road 383, just off of 247, a couple of miles north of the loop?"

"Maybe, it's been a while since I was out that way.

Wait, are you talking about the old oil company storage building, is it on the left?"

"I don't know. Yeah, it's on the left, old rusty metal, one of those huge Quonset huts or whatever. All the windows are broken out."

"I think I know where you mean. Is that where they are?"

"I don't know where they are. That's where they were camping. Promise you won't tell anybody. I mean anybody. Promise me." She spoke with urgency and fear.

"Priscilla, this may be too important for me to make a promise like that. I'll promise you this. I won't tell Rosie's family anything until I check it out, maybe talk to Rosie and Jimmy. OK?"

"Yeah, I guess. It's not like I didn't already tell you. I promised Rosie I wouldn't tell anyone, but I did." She sounded bitterly disappointed in herself.

"Hey, you just want them to be safe. That's more important than a promise not to tell."

"Whatever."

"Priscilla, you did the right thing. How did you know where they were?"

"Rosie told me the plan. I brought them some food and stuff. When I didn't hear from Rosie at all today, I decided to go check on them after school. The Tahoe is still there, but no sign of them."

"Did you search the area?"

"No. The place is creepy. I called out, but there was no answer."

"Were their things still there?"

"I don't know. They were camped in a back room. There are no lights or anything. I was afraid to look."

I sighed, and said, "OK. I'll check it out. There's probably nothing to worry about. If you hear from Rosie, give me a call."

After Priscilla hung up, I called Tony.

"Hey, 'copper,' are you up for an adventure?"

Once I had talked him into it, I gave him directions to the warehouse.

CHAPTER 9

"Jeepers, J.W., I nearly shot you." Tony's startled voice hissed out of the darkness in the abandoned warehouse.

"Shot me? You can't even see me. It's so dark you can't see your hand in front of your face."

"Not the point. Why didn't you stay with your truck?"

"There's something odd here. I couldn't see any light coming from inside the building. It's early enough you'd expect a lantern, candles or something. Also, its dead quiet in here."

"Did you have to phrase it like that?"

"I'm going to light up the night. Are you ready?"

"Wait. There's no power to this building. I checked. Have you got a flashlight?"

"No, I've got a one million candle power spotlight. Watch..."

I was holding the spotlight straight away from my body. When I pressed the switch, the brilliant beam illuminated a vehicle parked a little more than twenty feet in front of us.

The reflected light from the green Chevy pickup was just enough for me to see the look on Tony's face. He closed his eyes and took a deep breath. He opened his eyes and clenched his teeth for a moment.

"Stay here, I'll check it out."

"Hang on a minute, Tony. Let me shine the light around in here a little."

I maneuvered the beam around the inside of the building, spotting an open door at the far end. It looked like it went into what might once have been some sort of office. I swept the rest of the space and shone the light directly back onto the green pickup where it sat parked in the middle of the deserted warehouse.

"Watch my back." Tony said, as he walked toward the vehicle.

I held the spotlight steady as Tony circled the truck. He was careful to avoid looking in my direction. He waived me closer so he could see more clearly into the bed and the interior. I shone the beam through a side window as Tony peered carefully inside.

"Empty. They must have abandoned it here." He said.

"I need to save the battery. I'm going to turn off the light." I warned him.

The light faded, plunging us back into darkness. It took a moment for my eyes to adjust to the gloom. It was now easy to see the night time landscape outside, beyond the open bay through which we had both entered the building. Inside, we could see nothing.

"Let's go back to my car and call it in." Tony suggested.

"I think we should go have a look in that room at the end of the building."

"Why? If they were here, I'm pretty sure they'd have noticed that spot light. It's as quiet as a tomb in here."

"We have to check it out." I said.

"No, we don't. I can have a couple of uniforms here in about ten minutes."

"OK, you do that, while I go search the room."

I didn't have to see Tony's face to know what his expression would be.

"Hang on a minute." He said.

I could hear him fumbling around inside his jacket. I figured he was putting his gun away. In the sudden blue glow of his cell phone screen, Tony's face was as hard as stone.

"What are you gonna do, call dispatch and tell them you found an abandoned vehicle? I don't think that will get any priority attention."

"No, 'Sherlock'. I'm going to activate the flashlight app on my phone." Even as he uttered the words, the bright light stabbed me in the eyes. "That way we can walk over there and see what we're doing. You can shine your spotlight when we get there."

I had to admit it was a good idea. If I wasn't burdened by holding the big spotlight, I would've followed his example.

As we approached the room, each step was accompanied by the crunching of small bits of broken glass, and the sensation of walking on difficult to identify refuse. Tony mumbled, almost under his breath. "Oh man, this doesn't feel right."

I felt it too, an old familiar feeling, like a little cold worm shimmying up my spine. Maybe it was something about the air or maybe the hint of being in the presence of something foul.

Over the years, since this place shut down, kids had been coming here to party and homeless people occasionally camped out. There was no running water or any sanitation. The floor was littered with broken bottles and twenty years of filth. Nothing healthy had happened here in a very long time.

At the doorway I pointed the spotlight into the room and switched it on. The reflected light from the spotlight filled the room with a dull glow like a theater stage with the lights lowered, the intense beam brought into sharp focus each place where it came to rest. First an old metal shelf with some canned goods, bottled water and an ice chest. Next, a folding card table littered with fast food debris, and a battery powered lantern. Then, an ancient mattress on the floor, and on the mattress, something covered with a blanket.

"Over there, to the left." Tony directed.

I swung the beam to rest on a crumpled form in the corner. A dead man lay leaned against the wall, a shiny chrome revolver on the floor beside him.

Tony swore and started dialing his phone. His face looked drawn and waxy as he turned to me.

"I need you to clear out of here J.W. This is a crime scene."

"I won't come into the room, but you'd better have a look under the blanket on the mattress."

Tony spoke to me, "Stay right there," then into the phone, "This is Lieutenant Anthony Escalante, Robbery/Homicide. Put me through to Sergeant Ed Corcoran."

While he waited for the phone to be answered he walked over to the mattress and pulled a corner of the blanket back. "Ed, Tony, I'm on a crime scene. One white male approximately 20 years of age and a white female approximately 18 years of age, both deceased. It appears to be a homicide. Send everybody…"

I listened as he gave the address and location. When he had finished the phone call he walked back out of the room and turned to me. I pointed the spotlight down at the concrete floor, leaving us with enough reflected light to see each other.

"You should go now, J.W. We'll take it from here."

"Was it them?"

"I suspect so. It looks like they both died of gunshot wounds. We won't know anything for certain until we get some lights and forensics people in here to process the scene."

"Was it a murder-suicide?"

"Leave, J.W. Go out to your truck and drive away."

Tony's like that. Once he's on the job, he's all about police procedure. I knew he didn't have enough evidence or information to form an opinion and even if he did, he wouldn't tell me. Well, at least not right away.

"Do you want me to contact her parents?"

"No. We don't have a positive ID and it's my responsibility. Now, get out of here."

"OK. I'm gone. Thanks, Tony. I'm sorry it turned out this way."

"Yeah? Well, me too. I'll walk outside with you and wait for the troops to arrive."

When we were outside, I turned off the spotlight. As we stood there waiting for our eyes to adjust to the reduced light, Tony spoke up.

"Tell me, J.W. Had you already found the bodies?"

"What? No, of course not, I only got here about a minute before you did."

"But you knew what we'd find. It's why you called me."

Tony wasn't asking a question. He was stating a conclusion.

He deserved an honest response.

"I didn't know for sure, OK? I was just afraid it might be something like this. Rosie Ferguson's mother told me she had been in contact with a girl named Priscilla Davidson…"

"Rosie's best friend? Yeah, we interviewed her." Tony said.

"She failed to mention to the police that she's been in nearly constant contact with Rosie, texting back and forth, since she and Jimmy Duncan went missing. Priscilla even brought them food and money. When I talked to her about an hour ago, Priscilla told me they had been hiding here. She was really worried because Rosie hadn't been returning her texts since last night. She stopped by here this afternoon after school, saw the truck but no sign of Rosie or Jimmy. She said she was too scared to look in the back room."

"That makes her a suspect, J.W. At the very least she's an accessory after the fact."

"An accessory to what? She didn't have anything to do with what happened in that room, or even have any knowledge of it."

"She had knowledge of where the girl was being held and she withheld it from the police."

"Rosie wasn't being held. She was here with Jimmy because she wanted to be with him. Priscilla knew where Jimmy and Rosie were hiding. The important question, the question you should be asking is; who or what were they hiding from?"

CHAPTER 10

I called Hafsah Bashir at her hotel and arranged to meet her for breakfast at eight o'clock the next morning.

I found her waiting for me in the lobby.

Today, she wore blue jeans, tennis shoes and a burnt orange tee-shirt with a white longhorn symbol on it. Her hair was pulled back in a ponytail under a white UT ball-cap. She would easily pass for a Texas girl.

"Gig um Aggies." I said with a wink.

She looked confused for a moment. Her eyebrows lifted in question as she said, "Hook um horns?"

I grinned in response.

"Very impressive, you blend right in."

"Should we take our breakfast here in the hotel dining room?' She asked.

"That's fine with me. I don't like waiting in line to get into IHOP anyway."

She looked confused again.

"I hop? Is that hip hop? What does it mean to get into I hop?"

"Just kidding," I said, taking her elbow and guiding her toward the dining room.

As we lingered over our coffee, I observed there were only a few other people having breakfast in the dining room. With the clink of glassware, the canned music playing softly in the background and other ambient noise, I could hear other conversations, but I couldn't tell what people were saying. There was no one seated close to us, so I decided to get down to it.

"Do you keep your sidearm in your purse?" I asked.

"Excuse me?"

Where is your gun? You must have one on you somewhere. I couldn't spot it under your clothes."

"I beg your pardon!"

"Get over it. That offended attitude won't work on me, Hafsah.

"I do not know what you are talking about. Where would I acquire a firearm, and why would I want one?"

"… Any number of places between here and California. I expect your contacts in L.A. provided you with whatever you wanted. I know you are Mossad."

She locked eyes with me again. The depth in them was beckoning. I nearly fell in.

"You work rather fast. I am impressed." She said.

"You gave me all the right clues."

"Do you understand why I am here?"

"You're in pursuit of your cousin, Hakim Muktallah, right?"

"Yes, yes I am. How do you know this name?"

"It's one of the many names he's used. He did that murder in Barcelona about six weeks ago, didn't he?"

She looked away and nodded sadly. "He has killed many innocent people, in a number of places."

When she looked away, I was able to regain my wits. The thing is — I didn't want her to look away. I didn't want to talk business either. I wanted to get to know her, and I wanted her to see me, not as an ally or enemy, but as a man. Taking a deep breath, I re-focused.

"Why did you come to me?" I asked.

She returned her eyes to mine.

"I was told you are a skilled investigator and you had done work with your Department of Homeland Security. Before that you were a navy commando. What you call a SEAL, yes?"

"Mossad has a file on me?"

"So it would seem. Does it matter?"

"What else did they tell you?"

"Not so many things, some things which are difficult for me to understand."

"You do know I'm no longer working for our government?"

"Yes, that was another reason for choosing you. We do not have time to deal with the legal and bureaucratic restrictions your government would impose."

"… Why not? Israel and the U.S. are friends and allies."

She pursed her lips.

"Allies usually, yes that is so, but friends? I do not know. Not so much, not these days. Involving your government would cause delays and conflicts. We must find Hakim quickly. I failed in Barcelona. I will not fail again."

"This is how Mossad operates, I understand that, but Hakim is your cousin. Why did they task you with this assignment?"

"I requested the assignment. Everyone in Mossad knows he is my cousin. Hakim is dangerous and diabolical. It is a shameful thing for me to have a member of my own family, a terrorist, running around killing innocent people all over the world in the name of Allah."

"Tell me about your family, Hafsah."

"My father was Egyptian, my mother Lebanese, just as you surmised. I am an only child. Hakim is the son of my father's sister. She married a Saudi."

"How did you get recruited by Mossad?"

"My mother's family fled Beirut in the seventies when the civil war was becoming very bloody. They met and married in Egypt. My father's family was wealthy. After the death of my grandfather, my father came to manage the family's wealth. My parents were both well-educated and well-traveled. They were not fundamentalist Muslims. They tried to observe the five pillars of Islam, but not much more.

We lived a western lifestyle. I was young and impressionable. I had rejected Islam and was interested in philosophy and other religions. The late nineties were troubled times in Egypt, as they are now. My father sent me to attend university in Paris." She paused for a moment.

"It was there in Paris, both of my parents were killed in a café bombing while they were visiting me. I had gone to the lavatory. One moment in time saved my life. Had I not left the table when I did, I would have died with them.

That bombing was an act of Islamic terrorism. It was for me, the straw that broke the camel's back, as they say. I was approached by Mossad and I have been with them ever since."

"What is your religion, now?" I asked.

"My mother's family in Lebanon was Christian. My friends and associates in Mossad are mostly secular, very few are observant Jews. Our enemies are primarily Islamic. I fall on the secular side. I suppose I am agnostic."

"No, that isn't true. You know there is a God in heaven and He is the all in all."

She was silent for a moment. Her eyes got wide.

"Yes, I suppose I do. How do you know this about me?"

"I am His servant… and so are you."

"No, John. Please don't say that. Have we not heard enough from people who think they are servants of one god or another? The world does not need any more of that."

I shrugged.

"I understand. It seems to be an opinion that's growing in popularity. I hear someone saying the exact same thing, nearly every day, lately."

"I'm sorry. I do not mean to offend you, John. Your beliefs are your own business. I would simply appreciate it if you would not impose them on me."

"If we're going to work together, it's important we understand each other."

"Yes, it is." She agreed, once again meeting my eyes.

When she did that, looked into my eyes, it was as if we had always known each other. It was as if we always would. When she was looking into my eyes nothing else mattered.

"Where do you live?" I asked.

"I have a small villa in Italy, a pension in the Swiss Alps, an apartment in L.A., another in New York City, another in Paris and there is my family home in Alexandria. As I said, I am a woman of the world." She broke our eye contact.

"So you work for Mossad, but you don't live in Israel?"

"I seldom even visit in Israel. Because I am a businesswoman; I have activities that take me all over the world. Most of the time, I am traveling. So, I don't actually live anywhere. When Mossad has something I can help with, I do. Otherwise, my time is my own. The work I do for Mossad is clandestine. You are one of a very small number of people who have this knowledge. You will have to tell me exactly who told you about my involvement with them."

"In a way, you did."

"You may have gotten some idea, but someone has told you specifically. My work with Mossad is a well-kept secret. Who has told you this?"

"I can't say."

"Then why should I trust you?" She was angry, once again looking into my eyes.

I sensed there was more to the question than her words indicated.

"You know why."

She looked away again. "I suppose I have no choice."

"Trust is always a choice." I said.

She considered my comment for a moment, then changing the subject, she asked, "How do you see this search getting started?"

"I have some ideas. Tell me about this business of calling himself Nat Baha. Is he really a musician?"

CHAPTER 11

Nat Baha watched the six men crawling through the tall grass and weeds of the abandoned hay meadow. Each carried an assault rifle cradled in his arms. They crawled across the field, nearly pressed against the earth by the weight of the packs each man carried on his back.

These men only knew him by the name Nat Baha. Others knew him as Hakim Muktallah. He had used various names, but in every operation, he always assumed the persona of the man he was expected to be. Here, he was Nat Baha.

Today he trained his band of fighters in guerilla warfare techniques. Tonight, he and four of them would practice together as a band of skilled musicians. Each was important to Nat Baha and he would accept nothing less than the best effort from each man under his command. His plan required it.

He had chosen this part of the field because he knew it would be the most difficult to traverse. It was full of the plants the locals called sand burrs, sticker burrs or grass burrs. Whatever they were called, the dark brown seed pod was not much bigger than a BB, but there were at least a dozen per plant and each was covered with wickedly sharp and hardened barbs.

Also dotted here and there throughout the field, one could see the dirt mounds raised by the burrowing fire ants. He himself had made the mistake of standing too close to one of those mounds when he was being smuggled in from Mexico. The fire ants had swarmed up his legs and bitten him in scores of places. Each bite caused a stinging-burning pain that left him marked with tiny pustules at each location.

He had had to drop his pants and quickly brush the ants off his legs, stomping them as he loosened them from his socks and shoes. He had killed hundreds of the ants that day, stomping on them with his pants around his ankles, as the Coyote laughed at the spectacle.

It was the Mexican's last laugh.

"Enough! Assemble here." He called. It would do no good to exhaust the men or risk an injury that would interfere with their playing. It was approaching the time for the fourth prayers of the day.

The men climbed to their feet. They took a moment to pull the fabric of their pant legs away from where they were pinned to their knees, in the same way the sleeves of their jackets were pinned to their arms by the barbs of the grass burrs so prolific in this field. One by one they began to walk back over to where he stood in the shade of the giant sweet gum tree at the edge of the hay meadow. As they walked, each man was gingerly removing the burrs embedded into the flesh of their hands. The searing pain wasn't permanent, but it was intense. Their clothes were covered with the blackish burrs, each of which must likewise be picked off by hand. The grass burrs couldn't be removed without the men being stabbed in their fingertips in the process. The men winced and cursed as they walked toward him.

These men were all American citizens and Texans, either by birth or naturalization. All of them were familiar with the burrs and the fire ants. The point of the exercise was to toughen them and drive

home the importance of continued forward movement, while ignoring the pain.

Nat Baha considered Americans soft.

From the time he was a teenager he had lived in
camps and caves. He had fought beside men hardened by life in hostile environments. His chosen
life required that he endure great deprivation and
hardship.

None of these Americans had suffered what he had.
Yet, in all but one of them, he found a sincere dedication to the call of jihad. Other than the one exception,
these men were not posers or sycophants. They were
ready to fight and die for the cause of Allah.

Their hatred for the corrupt and depraved culture around them was hidden to their friends and
neighbors, but resolute within them. They were
committed to punish the American infidels for
the injustice they had allowed their government
to perpetrate against Muslim countries and people
around the world.

He nodded at the men now standing in line
before him.

"You are almost ready. This is good because the
time is at hand. Very soon now we will strike. Allahu Akbar!"

"Allahu Akbar! Allahu Akbar! Allahu Akbar!"
The men shouted in unison.

"Now my brothers it is time to prepare for Salat."
Nat Baha said.

****

At the core of Islamic life is adherence to the five
pillars of Islam as taught and demonstrated in the
life of the Prophet Muhammad – may his name be
honored forever. These five pillars begin with the
Shahada, the essential declaration that there is only
one god and Muhammad is his prophet. The second
pillar is the ritual prayers spoken five times a day,
called Salat. The third pillar is Zakat, the giving of

one's income to the poor and needy. The practice of fasting and self-control during the holy month of Ramadan is called Sawm. The fifth pillar, the Hajj, is making a pilgrimage to Mecca at least once in your life, if at all possible.

Because Salat must always be preceded by ritually washing the face, hands, and feet, Nat Baha dismissed the men to get cleaned up.

The old hay meadow was on the edge of the training camp. The camp consisted of a two-bedroom bunkhouse with a living area, kitchen and bathroom. Outside, a steel cargo container could be sealed against the weather or any kind of varmint. This was where the supplies and weapons were stored. There was also an old hay barn which was little more than a rusty steel frame with a corrugated metal roof. Because this had been a hunting camp there were three bunk beds in each of the bedrooms. Nat Baha lived here with one of the other men. The other trainees came and went to and from their homes and jobs. The barn was now used as an outdoor assembly hall, classroom and place of common prayer.

As the men rolled out their prayer mats, Nat Baha sang out the call to prayer, in Arabic.

"Allah is most great! I bear witness there is no god but Allah. I bear witness Muhammad is the prophet of Allah. Come to prayer. Come to wellbeing. Prayer is better than sleep. Allah is most great. There is no god but Allah!"

The Salat also involves bowing toward Mecca while reciting memorized prayers and sections of the Quran, spoken in Arabic. As the standing men got down on their still tender hands and knees, Nat Baha observed both their discomfort and their devotion. Before the next full moon, their true devotion would be put to the test.

CHAPTER 12

I was down on my hands and knees, waiving one of my sensors over an electrical outlet in the wall near her desk, when Christine came into the office.

"John, are you looking for a bug?"

I scowled at her and held my finger to my lips, indicating she should be quiet.

She rolled her eyes and shook her head.

"You've got to be kidding." She said.

When I had completed my sweep, concluding there were no listening devices in our offices that were not our own, I went back to the outer office to talk to her.

"Christine, I have something I need to tell you. This is so confidential; at first I was afraid to even tell you, at all. That's why I was sweeping the office. I'm still tempted to have this conversation somewhere else…"

"Then, let's do that," she said.

"Excuse me? I just swept the place. It should be OK."

"Should be, isn't good enough. Let's go get some coffee at Starbuck's or somewhere like that."

I pulled my head back.

"… Really?"

"Really, really, if there's something that important to talk about, let's not take any chances."

"I swear, you're becoming as paranoid as I am."

"Thank you, I'll take that as a compliment. Shall we?"

"Sure, why not."

We decided to drive over to the mall which was less than five minutes away. Once inside, we found a bench in the central courtyard. We could smell the odd mix of Chinese food, pizza, cookie dough and soft pretzels wafting from the nearby food court. With the fountain splashing behind us, we could sit close to each other and talk privately while dozens of people were moving all around, chattering to each other and paying no attention to us. It was as though our ordinary appearance wrapped us in a cloak of invisibility.

"This was a good idea." I admitted, quietly.

"Duh, I have those now and then you know. Besides, when you were sweeping the office, I'll bet you didn't check the most obvious weak point."

"And that is?"

"The security cameras are linked to our computers. They were watching us and recording everything we were saying. Did you get up into the ceiling to see if there was any kind of signal booster, or look for some kind of hack in thingy?" She asked.

"Hack in thingy?"

"You would know more about that than I do. It's possible isn't it?"

I slowly nodded in agreement.

"Yeah, it sure is, and so obvious, I can't believe I didn't even consider it."

"Well, that's sort of the whole point of hidden electronic surveillance, isn't it?"

I chuckled and grinned at her. "Pretty much, yeah, or so I've heard."

Christine smiled back.

"So, what is this big secret?"

"That's just it. It is a secret. You might even say its top secret."

Concern was now evident in her eyes. "Does this

have something to do with the CIA or the federal government?"

"No, not exactly, and… well, sort of."

"Then, I don't want to know anything about it." She held up a hand to stop me from speaking further.

"Christine, this is important and I don't want to hide anything from you."

"That's good enough for me. The less I know the better."

I thought about her statement for a moment. This was contrary to the way we did business. We always talked about every aspect of every case. I was stunned by her reluctance to be read in on the details of this one.

"Why? We don't keep secrets from each other. What's bothering you?"

"What's bothering me? Do I need to remind you of what happened the last time we were involved with a government agency? That was just the FBI. I don't want to have anything to do with spooks and spies. Nothing! Are we clear on that?"

"You'll understand if I behave strangely, or disappear for periods of time…"

"You do what you have to do, and I'll cover for you at the office."

"Christine, I…"

She held up her hand again.

"I trust you, John. Are you sure this is something you should be involved in?"

I looked at the floor for a moment. The loss of Gary was partially due to me trusting the wrong man. I had believed the FBI Special Agent would honor his promise to keep Gary safe. Now I was getting involved with another federal agency with close ties to the FBI. I understood her feelings. But this was a different case, and the lives of countless unknown people hung in the balance.

I nodded my head. "Yes, it is. I have to do this."

"Then do it to the glory of God." She said.

"OK, Thanks. I hear you."

"I mean it, John, I'll do whatever you need me to do, but I neither need nor want to know the details, OK?"

"That's more than I could've asked of you."

"Enough said. What can I do for you?"

"As you know, I'm trying to help Hafsa find her cousin. His name is Nat Baha, and he's a musician. He arrived here without his instrument, so he'll be looking for a guitar..."

"... Electric or acoustic?" she asked.

"He performs with an electric guitar, but he also plays acoustic. He's a jazz and bluesman, thinks he's the next Stevie Ray Vaughn. Can you imagine, a middle eastern bluesman?"

"So, you want me to research the local pawnshops and musical instrument stores, to see if he's shopping for a guitar?"

I nodded. "Exactly, and he may try to hook up with a recording studio or someone who can get him into a recording studio."

"Well, Tyler isn't Nashville or even Austin, but there are some places I can investigate. Willie Nelson and ZZ Top did some recording here."

"Really?"

"That's the rumor. Miranda Lambert is from Lindale, and there are several other professional musicians living in the area."

"I had no idea."

"That's because you don't get out much. You might want to consider taking Hafsah somewhere fun."

"We're not dating, she's just a client."

Christine looked me in the eye.

"That lady isn't 'just' anything, and I've seen the way you look at her."

"Christine..."

She held up her hand. "Ok, I'm just saying..."

When we stood up to leave, I saw the crowd around us with new eyes. These were colorful people shopping and socializing, acting out, checking each other out, and just getting on with their lives. Young and old, rich and poor, a multicultural mix of people, I sensed their vulnerability. Somewhere in the shadows, a predator lurked. Somewhere nearby a wolf was plotting the slaughter of these sheep, and the clock was ticking.

CHAPTER 13

I called Tony for an update on the mess I had left him with.

"Hey, Tony, I have to ask, did you make a positive identification of the shooting victims we found."

"Yes, we did. I'm sorry, J.W. It's bad news."

"Have you notified the girl's parents?"

"Yes. It was my unfortunate duty to tell them their daughter and her supposed abductor, were both deceased."

"I wonder why they didn't call me? Wait a minute. You said 'supposed abductor'. You know Jimmy Duncan didn't take Rosie against her will. Was it a murder suicide?"

"Officially, this department is conducting an investigation into the cause of death. Off the record, J.W., I'm investigating it as a double homicide."

"So, it wasn't a murder-suicide?"

"No, but it was staged to look that way. The girl was shot where we found her on the mattress. The man was shot where we found him, but he didn't do the shooting."

"How do you know that?"

"We found Jimmy Duncan's prints on the revolver we recovered at the scene, but only on the grip and trigger. The rest of the gun's exposed surface didn't have a print on it, not even a smudge."

"Somebody wiped it and put it in his hand."

"Five'll get you ten. Then there's the fact there was no powder residue on Duncan's hands or sleeves. We found residue on his upper chest. He was killed with a single gunshot — point blank under his chin, up through the top of his head. There's powder burn under his chin. The residue on his chest is consistent with where the gun would've been when it was fired, but he didn't fire it."

"The evidence would suggest that, but you can't be certain."

"Well, there's more. The lab found fingerprint smudges on the cylinder where it didn't get wiped down and there are prints and partials on the cartridges. Those prints don't match the victim."

"That's good work, Tony."

"Thanks, we do what we can. All that tells us is someone else did the shooting. It doesn't tell us who."

"Are you going to question Priscilla Davidson?"

"Already did. She was grief stricken at the news. The coroner put the time of death at about 24 hours before we arrived on the scene. Priscilla was on stage in a school play at that time. Prior to that, she was at her after school job, before that, school. Her alibi is rock solid. So, she's in the clear, J.W."

"Hang on a second. You said you only told Rosie's parents that you had found the bodies. Did you tell them the circumstances? Do they know where it happened? Did they ask you if it was a murder-suicide?"

"Huh, can't think of any questions, can you? No, they haven't been informed of any of the specifics, including the location of the shooting. As for asking if it was a murder-suicide, Mr. Ferguson as much as told me it was. Maybe they assumed it. I didn't correct their assumption."

"Why not?"

"You told me Rosie and Jimmy were hiding from someone. You suggested I should try to find out who they were hiding from. That's what I'm working on. It wouldn't be appropriate to reveal all we know at this time, would it?"

"No, it wouldn't. You're on the right track, Tony. You might want to interview Priscilla again. She's keeping secrets."

Tony sighed into the phone.

"What's the point? We already know she didn't do it."

"Do you have any suspects?"

"Of course, we have suspects."

"Do you have enough evidence to make an arrest?"

"No, we can't tie the gun to anyone, there were no witnesses, and the crime scene had too much accumulated debris and DNA to provide any useful data. It's a case of too much information."

"That's why you need to interview Priscilla again. You need to know what she knows."

"Right, I hear you. She's keeping secrets — a dead girl's secrets."

"It goes to motive, Tony"

"Do you think she'll tell the police what she knows?"

It was my turn to sigh.

"OK, let's do it together. I'm pretty sure she'll talk to me. I'll set it up."

CHAPTER 14

DHS agent Jack McCarthy met me on the top level of the parking garage at Olympic Plaza. I arrived before he did. He wasn't late; I just like to be the first person on the scene, rather than the last.

The top level was reserved for staff, but there was no one checking. After he parked next to me, Jack climbed into the passenger seat of my truck which I had running with the AC blowing.

"How can you stand living in this heat?" He asked.

"It's not the heat. It's the heat and the humidity."

"Whatever. It's got me looking forward to winter. Speaking of looking forward, I brought you the pertinent data we have on the people we suspect may be planning an attack." He dropped a file folder on my console. "All of these guys are American citizens and none of them have committed a crime, yet. We've been expecting trouble from them, but now that Muktallah is here, we think it could be much worse than anticipated. Our analysis suggests the probability of a devastating, mass casualty terrorist incident."

I decided not to ask how he arrived at a conclusion about what I might think was pertinent.

"I thought the word "terrorist" was unpopular these days. Aren't you government types supposed to say "act of violence" or something like that?"

"We don't have time for your cynicism, John."

"Do you know if any of them were in contact with Muktallah?"

"No, we don't think they ever had any direct contact with him. We suspect he was sent by someone without any of the locals knowing he was coming."

"How did you get onto these guys?"

"We gathered most of our intelligence from electronic surveillance and confirmed it through various other channels. We learned a lot about them from the internet sites they were visiting on the dark web. We knew one of them was in touch with an Imam in Yemen who is also a low level Al Qaeda footman. Another guy made a similar connection on a trip to Pakistan, and one traveled to Syria and he's stayed in contact with ISIS fighters since then. That's probably the connection to Muktallah. It's all there in the file."

"I don't understand how this could happen here. The local Muslims have never been a problem, Jack. The little area mosque has always reached out to the community and many of the people are well respected here. They are charitable people who are committed to the five pillars of Islam. How in the world did they get involved in all this radical jihadist madness?"

"We're not talking about all of the local Muslims. It has nothing to do with the mosque. We're talking about a very few people who are mostly self-radicalized. These are people who would be radical if they belonged to the girl scouts or an association of librarians. They're just wired that way."

"Wired to bring jihad to the streets of America?"

"I'm afraid so. For millions of people it's possible to be a Muslim but not a serious Islamist. They're culturally Muslim, practicing the primary tenants and traditions of the religion, without any political agenda. But the person who is truly committed to Islam is committed to the entire Islamic agenda. Islam is both a religion and a political system. A radical Islamist cannot stand to see the interference of infidels in the politics of the Islamic countries. They can't stand to see the nation of Israel occupying any part of the Middle East. They hate Americans because we've made war on Islamic people in Islamic countries, and we support Israel. They intend to punish us for these things. That's the rationale for jihad. They will never stop.

One day they hope to see the whole earth under the thumb of Islam. It's been the goal since the time of Muhammad. It's part of the reason for the continual upheaval throughout the Middle East. What started as strife between tribes and factions within the region has gone global. Today, the radicals are ascendant. Have you got any leads on where Muktallah might be?"

"You've been watching these guys. He's probably with one of them. Where do they live? Who visits them? Who do they visit? You know the drill, Jack. You should have found him yourself by now."

"Well, we haven't. He's a ghost. Sure, we're watching the men in that file. We've followed each of them everywhere they go. Do you have any idea how many man hours I'm talking about? A couple of them are in a band. They get together and practice. They have jobs, go to school, one of them owns a machine shop. They lead fairly boring lives. I've got a lot on my plate. What have you got?"

"I know you aren't telling me everything. How long have you been watching them?"

"I told you, we picked up some signals that suggested they were becoming radical. This was about three months ago. We started our surveillance, trying to gather any useful intel we could. They're just smart enough not to talk to strangers, so the agent we sent to try to lure them out in the open got a cold shoulder. Our analysts are certain they're a threat, but we can't prove it. Now they're being trained by a pro. So, what are you and your little friend doing to help us?"

I ignored his condescending attitude.

"Hafsah is going to return to her Islamic roots and try to make herself part of the local Muslim community. I'm helping with some introductions. Now that we have this list, she'll be able to focus her attention on these people. We're also working another angle. It's just going to take time, and I don't think we have much of it."

"No, I'm afraid we don't have the luxury of a cushion of time. The clock is ticking and about to chime. What is this other angle you mentioned?"

"It turns out Muktallah actually is a musician. He's a jazz and bluesman. He wants to make a record. It must be funny to him that he can come here illegally and plan to do violence against innocent people and record American music at the same time."

"You're kidding? We never heard anything about any of that. Are you sure?"

"Yeah, strange isn't it?"

"These are strange times, John."

CHAPTER 15

Hafsah and I sat in my office and looked through the file Jack had given me.

She had donned traditional Muslim clothing. Today she wore an ankle length dress with long sleeves and a high bodice. It was lavender, with a subtle floral print. A white hijab of opaque silk was now draped around her shoulders. Before going out in public she would pull it up over her head and pin it under her chin. To me she looked like any of the other Muslim women I had seen on the streets in many parts of the western world. Like them, but much more beautiful.

"How did you come to have this dossier?" She asked.

I had been expecting this question.

"I got it from a friend in the Department of Homeland Security. I asked him to do some research for me. These are local people who've drawn the attention of our government as being potential trouble makers."

"Did your friend not question you about your interest in these people?"

"He did. I told him someone who might be a Muslim had made some threats against one of my clients, and I just wanted to know if there was a reason to be concerned."

"How is it that he was so willing to give you this information?"

"As I said, he's a friend. He knows I won't use the information inappropriately. I just thought it might be helpful. Maybe someone in this group has some connection with your cousin. What do you think?"

"I think your inquiry will draw the attention of your government. You may have alerted the FBI."

"OK, I can handle that. Again, do you think someone in this group might be in contact with your cousin?"

I could see she wanted to have a look at the file.

"Yes, it is possible. If Hakim knows someone here, it would probably be in the Muslim community. Are any of these people involved with the music industry?"

"I have no idea, besides — do you really think Hakim came here to make a record of his music? He could make a record anywhere in the world."

Hafsah met my eyes.

"No, John, we both know he did not sneak into your country just to make music. He is here to make war on your people, in the name of Allah. He is here to kill and terrorize your people." She paused, looking away. "There it is. I followed him here to find him and kill him before he commits one more atrocity."

Leaning forward, I took her hands in mine.

"I've known it from the first time I met you. Is it so easy for you to speak of killing someone?"

She shook her head, but didn't pull her hands away.

"You must try to understand. He is not just some random person. He is a killer, an assassin who has come here to kill many of your people. I must stop him. I am prepared to do whatever is necessary to accomplish this. If he realizes I am his enemy, he will kill me without hesitation. I cannot hesitate either. If I hesitate, I will die, and he will be free to go on killing many more people. This is not a contest or a prizefight. It is not even a… how do you say, bar fight? This is a fight to the death and only one of us will survive. Do you understand?"

"Yes, I do, but if we can capture him, will you do that, instead?"

"I do not think you understand this man. I do not think you can imagine a man so evil. It is the weakness of you Americans. You always try to see the best in people and you put so much pride in your criminal justice system.

Some people are evil. Hakim is not an ordinary criminal. He is a terrorist. He is dedicated to Jihad, the holy war. For him, killing the enemies of Islam is his personal calling. He believes he is following the example of the Prophet. Any country or any citizen of a country that has opposed any aspect of Islam is to be cut off. He is the enemy of every man, woman and child in your homeland. He is here to kill innocent civilians, striking at the heart of your American values.

If he learns you are hunting him, he will kill you, John. He will not hesitate or even give it more than a passing thought. He intends to kill as many people as he can before he falls. You would be just one more..."

I put my hand up, stopping her.

"I do understand, Hafsah. Don't be afraid for me. I have more experience in these things than you can imagine. Like you, I know the best weapon we have is our mind. If we are mentally prepared to stop our enemy by any means necessary, before he harms us, only then can we win. If we allow an enemy to put us on the defensive, we only have a fifty-fifty chance of survival. I've never liked those odds.

Listen to me. If the only way we can stop him is by killing him, I'll do it myself. I won't hesitate either. That being said, if God is willing, we will take him alive."

"Why alive? Do you intend to turn him over to your authorities?"

"Yes, but that isn't the only reason."

She scowled, trying to work out another reason. This was outside her experience and understanding.

"It's not too late for him, Hafsah. He can be redeemed."

Hafsah huffed, expressing her disdain for the notion.

"Redeemed? No, he deserves death. He is beyond redemption."

"We all deserve death, but God is rich in mercy. If we can take him alive, will you help me do that?

"Inch' Allah." She shrugged.

"Does he know you are coming for him, Hafsah?"

"He must know he is being hunted. That is why he cannot travel openly. There is nowhere he can go where someone will not be hunting him. He knows he has little time left. It is why he has this crazy idea about making a recording of his music. I do not think he knows anything about me. He probably would not remember me even if we met face to face. We have not seen each other since we were children. He does not know I am Mossad."

It was good news to me. It meant even if they met by chance somewhere in the area, he would not suspect her of being anything other than a local Muslim woman.

"OK, I think the first person we need to find is this guy, Jahander Khalid. He's a student at the university. The fall semester is just starting. I'll do some research and get his class schedule. You can bump into him on campus, saying you're there visiting a friend you met in France and you're considering taking a teaching assignment. Christine can pose as the friend if we need her to."

"Does he have a sister or a girlfriend? It would be better to meet her first. Perhaps I should not be so forward introducing myself to him. It might seem odd and provoke his suspicion."

"Uh, I don't know. There is nothing about it in this file. I'll have to look into it."

"Is there another person who might be contacted more easily?" She asked.

I handed her another photograph. "We could try this guy. He works at a convenience store in Jacksonville, a town about fifteen miles south of here."

"Yes? I will go there and buy petrol. Perhaps he

will ask me where I come from."

"Do you happen to speak any Pashtu?"

"I do, yes. Why do you ask?"

"This guy's family comes from the tribal region on the Afghan border. He visited there last year. He probably learned to speak Pashtu."

"What is his name?"

"It says here he goes by Aaron Parviz. He's lived in the U.S. since he was four years old. Hello… this is interesting. He plays the drums in a band called the Honky Tonk Broncs."

"What does this mean "honky tonk Bronx"? I know the Bronx, and the other four boroughs of New York City. They are Manhattan, Brooklyn, Queens, and…"

I stopped her, shaking my head.

"… No, it's not about… the point is he's a musician. He's the sort of person Hakim would want to know."

"Have I told you I am a musician as well?" She asked.

It had never crossed my mind.

"No, what do you play?"

"… Strings. I play violin, cello and piano, primarily."

"Wow. I had no idea. Are you any good?"

She slapped me on the shoulder.

"It is a matter of opinion. Some people think I am capable."

"Oh, of course, I mean… I'm sorry. I didn't phrase the question correctly."

She grinned at me.

"I have performed with professional musicians on two continents."

"Really? That is impressive."

"Do you play?"

"I have a huge playlist. I play a wicked stereo, even on my car audio system."

She blinked and tilted her head to one side, perplexed.

"No, I have no musical talent, whatsoever." I clarified.

She smiled and said, "Perhaps, someday I will play for you…"

"Please, God?" I breathed a silent prayer.

CHAPTER 16

"I have news." Christine informed me, as I came in the front door of our office, that afternoon. "Two days ago, Ace Pawn and Jewelry sold a classic Fender Stratocaster and an amplifier for cash, nearly two thousand dollars in cash, to a guy named Nat Baha. He was looking for a very specific guitar, and they had one."

"Bingo! Did they get an address?"

"No, he paid in cash, but he was looking to buy some additional equipment, Ace didn't have. He left a phone number in case something he wanted came in."

She handed me a piece of paper with the number on it.

"Probably a throwaway phone," I speculated.

"Well, thank you so much for that word of encouragement," she said.

I grinned.

"Sorry Christine. You did great, faster and better than I could have imagined. Thank you."

"I guess you don't have much imagination, do you?"

"Why do you say that?"

"What if Nat Baha got a call from the pawnshop, saying they had something he was looking for?"

"And what if we were in a position to follow him from the pawnshop?"

"Why do you want to follow him? I thought you

just wanted to find him."

"Right, I did. Just a slight change of plans, don't give it another thought."

"Hmm," Christine replied, narrowing her eyes.

"Keep on the recording angle, too. OK?"

"Yes, boss."

"Thank you."

"Uh huh. What about the equipment?" She asked.

"What equipment?"

"I told you, Nat Baha is looking for some sort of special distortion thingy, a foot pedal thingy and some other stuff."

"Did you write it down, too?"

"Here you go," she said, handing me another piece of paper.

I scanned the list. It was all strange to me.

"What is a 'Vox Wah'? Did I even say that right?"

"You did. It's an old school reverb kind of thingy. It distorts the sound as you step on the foot pedal. I have someone locating one now. We can provide it to the pawnshop, and 'voila' along comes Nat Baha to pick it up."

"Excellent, I like your plan."

"I thought you would. Apparently they aren't hard to find, so we should be able to pull it together pretty quickly."

"Great. Let me know when you know."

"Where is Hafsah?"

"She went to Jacksonville."

"Jacksonville, Texas, whatever for?"

"… To get gas."

Christine waited for me to elaborate.

I shrugged.

"It's a long story. I think she said something about meeting someone she might know there."

"Uh huh."

"Let it go, Christine."

She gave me a smug look as I turned to walk away.

"I can if you can." She said.

CHAPTER 17

As I drove into the parking lot of Hafsah's hotel, I observed a man standing outside the front entrance smoking a cigarette. I parked and walked back toward the entrance. The smoker was no longer there.

In the lobby, a couple seated in the reception area glanced at me as I made my way to the bank of elevators.

I found room 314 and knocked on the door.

A moment later, Hafsah, wearing a light blue, full length caftan with a floral pattern in gold embroidery and flared sleeves, answered my knock. Her dark hair was loose and fell in swirls to her shoulders. Her flawless makeup was still in place.

She smiled with genuine delight upon seeing me, and putting her hands on my shoulders, she greeted me with the traditional kiss on both cheeks. It evoked memories of how long it had been since a woman had kissed me. Her hair was lightly scented with a delicate perfume. The scent couldn't have been any headier to me if she had bathed in it. It took all the restraint I had in me to stop myself from taking her in my arms and kissing her with somewhat greater passion than might be considered a traditional greeting.

She took my hand and led me into her suite.

"John, is there something troubling you?"

"It's just another case I'm working on. I don't like where it's leading. I've pulled a friend into an ugly situation. I usually watch his back."

She considered my answer for a moment. I could tell she was thinking through her response. She squinted at me.

"Why would you wash his back?"

I chuckled. "To watch someone's back, means to provide protection from an unknown threat they might not see coming. It's a jargon expression or idiom."

She looked amused, a little smile forming at the corners of her mouth.

"Is that so? I never knew that. You should not have let the cat out of the bag."

I laughed, she had set me up and I walked right into it.

"Gotcha!" She said. "Would you care for a drink? Perhaps some wine?"

"I'll have whatever you're having."

Soon we were settled in the sitting area with glasses of Pinot Noir.

Hafsah sat on the couch with her legs drawn up under her. I sat in an easy chair opposite her with the little coffee table between us.

I couldn't help admiring her shape and the way the caftan stretched across her thigh. It was painfully evident she wasn't hiding a gun... or much of anything else.

She caught my eyes.

"Let me tell you about my trip to the town of Jacksonville," she said. "I drove to the convenience store referenced in the dossier. I went inside to present the cashier with payment before I filled the vehicle's tank with petrol..."

I found myself smiling at her phrasing.

"...I immediately recognized the clerk as being our subject - Aaron Parviz. He was very friendly, seeing me as a Muslim woman. He asked where I was from, and I told him I was visiting Tyler, from Los Angeles, but I had been born in Islamabad. He told me he had also been born there and had recently visited Pakistan. Some of his family is still living in the Waziristan region. I spoke the traditional greeting to him in Pashtu. He responded with obvious surprise and pleasure."

"Well done," I said, interrupting her for a moment.

"I then returned outside and fueled the automobile. When I came back into the building, I made small talk and admired a set of drums over in a corner of the store. He told me they were his and he practiced on them when there were no customers.

I nodded my encouragement.

"I asked him if he was in a band or musical group. He told me he was in a band called the 'Honky Tonk Broncs', and he showed me a poster on the wall."

"Very well done," I observed.

"Umm," she agreed. "I pretended to be impressed by this. He seemed very excited by my interest. He went on to tell me the Honky Tonk Broncs are to be an opening act in an upcoming concert here in Tyler. The headliner is someone named Kyle Coltrane. Do you know this name, John?"

"I do, yes. I heard it mentioned just recently. I guess he's sort of famous in the popular music business."

Hafsah shrugged. "So I gathered. Aaron Parvis asked me if I would be interested in attending the concert, indicating he might be able to 'get me in'. I told him I worked for a record producer named Earl Hightower who might be interested in hearing the band play. He seemed enamored with me. I believe he was attempting to discover whether or not I have a 'significant other'. Is that the correct expression?" She asked shyly.

"I reckon so." I drawled.

"He told me his name and I introduced myself using the name Nadia Ahmed."

"How do you keep track of all the false names you use?" I asked.

"I do it the same way you do. It is an acquired skill, John." She smiled.

"Indeed, it is."

"Does it bother you?"

I took a deep breath. In this war, I've used several different names, some for my work, some for my life, in both this century and the last. Her use of a false name didn't bother me at all. I had given her my favorite alias. I had even supplied her with some of my fancy embossed business cards that just had the name "Earl Hightower" and a phone number on them. There was something entirely different, though not unrelated, we needed to discuss. I figured now was as good a time as any for me to bring it up.

"No, Hafsah. What troubles me is the fact that you have other Mossad agents here with you, and you haven't bothered to mention it."

Her eyes widened and she nearly spilled her wine.

"How did you know? Who told you?"

"I didn't know, for sure, until you just confirmed it."

She closed her eyes, those oh so beautiful eyes.

"I am sorry, John. We are in the practice of being discrete. I did not think you needed to know." She said, urgently leaning forward to engage me. "I mean it, John, I am truly sorry."

"Yeah, well sorry don't cover it. How many are there and what is their purpose?"

She took a deep breath.

"There are four of us, in total. We are two women and two men. I am the lead agent. The other three are support and logistics specialists. They also handle communications and provide security for me. How did you spot them?"

"I first saw them in the dining room, that first morning. I saw them again tonight. It's what I do."

"Yes, you are very good. I know I should have told you from the beginning."

"Trust is a choice, Hafsah."

"You must try to understand, John. I didn't tell

you because I am not permitted to do so. It was not about trust. Mossad has a certain way of doing things. I am just a servant, not the master."

I smiled and touched her cheek.

"I do understand. I am a servant myself, remember?"

Hafsah took my hand in hers and searched my eyes.

"John, please understand. I had no intention of deceiving you. If you want to meet the other members of my team, I will call them in here."

"No. It might be better if they don't know that I know. One of them would inform your superiors. That could create some unforeseen complications. Don't you think?"

She was thoughtful for a moment.

"Will you tell your superiors?" She asked, watching me closely.

"Hafsah, I'm not working for any government agency. I'm helping you because you came to me. I don't have to report this to anyone."

"That is good. I am sorry, but I had to ask the question."

I decided to give her some encouragement.

"Let me tell you what I've learned. My associate, Christine, has discovered a guy by the name of Nat Baha purchased an electric guitar, an amplifier, and some other things at a local pawnshop, two days ago. He's looking for additional equipment they didn't have. Christine is going to arrange to have the pawnshop call Mr. Baha and tell him they now have that equipment."

Her jaw firmed and fire came into her eyes.

"Do you know where he is staying?" she asked, excitedly.

"No, he paid for the things he bought with cash and only left a phone number." I handed her the slip of paper with the number written on it. "I expect it's a throwaway phone, but you can have your team check it out."

"Thank you, this is excellent. We will set up surveillance on the pawnshop. We may be able to take Hakim when he shows up for the rest of the equipment."

"No, we have additional fish to gather in the net. I know you are only tasked with getting your cousin, Hafsah, but I want to stop the whole bunch of them. Hakim came here to lead an attack. Eliminating him might delay the attack, but it wouldn't stop it."

"That is not my mission, John. I must stop Hakim, by any means necessary and at the first opportunity."

"Hafsah, listen to me. Many lives are at stake here. We have a chance to stop a terrorist attack, and get Hakim in the process. He's been here long enough to organize these men and plan an attack on a specific location. If we just take Hakim, it won't stop the attack. Can you let that happen?"

I could see she was struggling with the question.

"I will have to ask my superiors for direction in this matter."

"I don't think so, Hafsah. I'm not asking your handlers in Tel Aviv or Jerusalem for anything. I'm asking you. Will you help me stop the attack from ever happening?"

She looked deeply into my eyes. After a moment she nodded.

"Yes, John. We will stop it together."

I chuckled. "We are quite a pair. Each of us wanting to trust the other, but each a product of our training."

"Sadly, yes. But, John, I want you to know I have grown very… fond of you. I would never deliberately do anything to hurt you…" she trailed off.

"…And I you, but you already know that, don't you?"

She smiled brightly. "I was hoping it was so!"

We held each other's hands for a moment. The desire to kiss her was nearly overwhelming me.

She must have sensed my inclination, and shared it, because she met me halfway.

As we kissed, I was aware she could be trying to seduce me and use my male weakness to manipulate me. Could be, but I believed in her sincerity, and I was sensitive to her own vulnerability. I didn't completely lose my head, but I was nearly overwhelmed by the sheer sensuality of the moment.

When we both came up for air, Hafsah's eyes were twinkling with delight. I found myself grinning like the Cheshire cat! I felt like I was sixteen years old again. Astonishing, considering the year I was born.

That thought brought me back to earth with a horrendous impact.

CHAPTER 18

As the men were sharing the evening meal, Aaron Parvis spoke up.

"I met a fascinating Muslim woman at the store today."

"Hah! To you, all women are fascinating," said his friend, Jahander Khalid.

"Well, pretty much, yeah," Aaron said. The two men grinned at each other. "But this woman has just moved here from L.A., and she speaks Pashtu."

The other men at the table now gave him their full attention.

"Now you're talkin', a California girl! What does she look like?" Jahander asked?

"She's beautiful. Dark eyes and complexion, a brilliant smile…"

"How about her body? Is she a ten, or a hen?"

"I sure wouldn't kick her out of bed."

"Hah! As if you could get her into one."

"Enough of this lewd talk!" Nat Baha slapped his hand on the table. "Is this woman married?"

"No, she's single. I think she might've been flirting with me."

"You think every woman is flirting with you," said Jahander.

Nat Baha scowled and said, "You say she is Muslim. Is she a woman of virtue, or a typical Western-ized whore?"

"I believe she is devoted to the Prophet — may his name be forever adored. Her appearance was very traditional, in both dress and manner."

"Then do not speak of her so disrespectfully. What is her name?" asked Nat Baha.

"Nadia Ahmed. And get this, she works for a guy in the music business."

Nat Baha sat up straight.

"How did you come to meet this woman?" He asked.

"She's just a customer. She was buying gas."

"Who does she work for?"

"She says his name is Ed, or maybe Earl-some-thing. Evidently he's some kind of music producer or talent recruiter."

"Did you not ask her for more details?"

"Well, uh, no. I was more interested in her. She seemed pretty excited about the concert, though."

As the conversation moved on to other things, Nat Baha considered what Aaron had told them. Was meeting this woman just a random encounter, a divine portent, or something more sinister? Perhaps it was nothing more than an interesting coincidence.

Nat Baha didn't believe in coincidence. He broke into the light hearted banter.

"Did you tell this woman… what did you say her name is?"

"… Nadia Ahmed, from California."

"Did you tell Miss Ahmed that you will be per-forming with the band at the concert?"

"Yep. I offered to get her in. She said she would discuss it with her boss. Maybe he'd be interested in seeing us play."

Nodding, Nat Baha said nothing further. As he mulled over the possibilities he stroked his beard, watching the men at the table. The lead guitar player, Jeff Tolbert was a problem. The others had vouched for him, saying Tolbert had recently converted to

Islam. Baha didn't trust him. Why had the man not selected a Muslim name? He was training well enough, but was he a true Muslim? The man's skills were only marginal. Could he be counted on when the killing began? No, there was something amiss.

Nat Baha felt the presence of the angel and as he opened his mind to the unheard voice, he knew then what must be done.

Jeff Tolbert would not be missed.

CHAPTER 19

I was a little late getting to the office the next morning. Christine was already seated at her desk, wearing a striped sweater in forest green and black, with silver jewelry. She had her shining red hair loosely braided and pulled forward over one shoulder. She looked up from her computer screen as I approached her desk.

"I have some bad news, John. I arranged to have the pawnshop call Nat Baha about the foot pedal thingy. He told them he had already gotten all the equipment he needed."

"The Vox Wah, wah," I said.

"Wah, wah, wah." She said, making a sad face.

I had to smile.

"That is bad news. It was such a good lead and pretty much our only lead."

"Well, maybe not our only lead. I've been researching local recording studios and other places where musicians gather. Sure enough, a guy by the name of Nat Baha has been asking around about setting up a recording session."

"Outstanding! Tell me more."

"He wants to record a heavy blues guitar session. He appears to be shopping prices. As you know, getting a record made is as easy as pie, if you have enough money. Getting it reproduced, promoted, marketed, shipped and sold is a whole different story. It takes industry connections and some very deep pockets."

As usual, Christine's observation was critical. I hadn't even considered the cost.

"What would it cost to get a demo record made?

"I don't know. What with studio rental, paying sound technicians, and whatever else, probably at least a few grand. All that would get you is a single CD and maybe a digital version of the recording. You could carry it around with you and play it for your friends. If you wanted to do anything commercially productive with it, you'd need an agent to get it in the hands of the movers and shakers. You know, get it to someone who could make a real record and promote you as an artist. Nobody would ever hear your music, without someone promoting it."

"I guess it's like a lot of other things, you get what you pay for. I imagine there are many different ways to get all that done." I speculated.

"Sure, but if you do it yourself, they're all incredibly expensive. The best way is the traditional way. Get a recording contract with a reputable record company. That way, the company bears all the up-front cost and risk. They have everything in place from providing studio space, a producer, sound technicians and studio musicians, to promotion and marketing people, whatever it takes to produce a successful and profitable record. They can even handle concert booking and travel arrangements."

"Yeah, but our boy doesn't have a recording contract. He'll have to pay for everything himself, studio musicians, sound technicians, getting the CDs, packaging, shipping, advertising, the whole nine yards."

"He's been telling people he has his own back-up band, so he won't need studio musicians."

"That won't save him much money, and he still won't have any name recognition or ready-made market for his recording." I mused.

"Do you know if he's some kind of millionaire? It will cost many thousands of dollars to do all that, unless he develops some name recognition." Christine said.

… Name recognition. Could he be thinking once he was identified as an international terrorist, responsible for mass murder in the U.S. and other countries, people would want to buy his record to hear his music? I didn't think so. He wanted people to hear his music as soon as possible, before he became known as one of the most twisted people in history.

"No, he's burned through a lot of money, probably family money, but he isn't wealthy at all. I think he's running low on cash." I said.

"Well then, he must have some sort of plan we don't know about." She replied.

"Yes, I imagine he does. Thanks, Christine. You're on the right track to finding him. Please make it your first priority."

"It already is, John. You've made that very clear. Besides, I'm pretty curious about this guy myself."

I had a thought.

"Christine, you follow the local music scene, have you ever heard of a local band called the Honky Tonk Broncs?"

"You're kidding, right? Did you read this morning's paper? The Broncs are becoming the best known band in the Ark-La-Tex. They're supposed to be the opening act for Kyle Coltrane, this weekend."

"How is that newsworthy?"

"Obviously you didn't read the paper. Jeff Tolbert, the lead guitarist for the Broncs, just committed suicide."

What an interesting turn of events. Some would say a coincidence. I don't believe in coincidence. This would require further investigation.

"Christine, do you know anyone connected with the band?"

"No, but I can make some inquiries. All the members live here in the area. They're expected to break out and start touring, maybe with Kyle Coltrane. This is a lousy time to lose their lead guitarist. What do you want to know?"

"Nothing, right now, let it go. I was just curious."

"Uh uhh, I know you better than that. You're never just curious." She narrowed her eyes at me.

I shrugged in response.

"Ok, out with it. Why are you asking?" She demanded.

"Well, I was thinking about taking Hafsah to the concert on Saturday, and wanted to maybe, you know, get good tickets and maybe a backstage pass..."

Christine lit up like the Eiffel Tower at the stroke of midnight on New Year's Eve, all smiles and twinkling eyes.

"Wahoo! I knew it! You bet, John. I don't know anybody connected with the Broncs, but I know the concert promoters. I'll make it happen."

"Really, you can do that?"

"Leave it to me. We could double date. Tony and I were planning to go Saturday night, anyway."

"Yeah? I think Hafsah would like that."

"You should give Tony a call, and tell him about your plans."

"OK, I'll do it. It's not exactly a slow news day, huh?" I observed.

Christine just shook her head.

I called Tony.

"Hey J.W., what's the buzz?" He asked, by way of greeting.

"Nothing new, how's the fuzz?"

"Ouch, was that a derogatory reference to my employment in public service as a peace officer? I'll have you run in and we'll take the rubber hose to you."

"What if I give you donuts?"

"... Donuts? Yeah, cops like donuts."

We both laughed.

"Listen, Christine and I were talking. She tells me you and she are planning to go to the Kyle Coltrane concert on Saturday. I was wondering if I could join you, and bring a date."

"Yeah, Christine has an in with the concert promoters, so... Wait a minute. Did you say 'bring a date'?"

"Yep."

"You? You have an interest in a girl?"

"Woman, Tony. It's socially unacceptable and politically incorrect to say 'girl'. Besides, why act so surprised?"

"Who's acting?"

"So, I take it you have no objections."

Tony laughed.

"No, of course not, it should be a really good time."

"Listen, the opening act is a band called the "Honky Tonk Broncs. I understand the lead guitar player for the band is recently deceased..."

"... Oh boy, here we go." Tony said."

"The paper says it was an apparent suicide. Has the coroner confirmed it?"

Tony was quiet for a moment. Finally he spoke up, his voice subdued.

"You always do this. I swear, I should expect it, but I never do."

"Do what?"

"I have the report in front of me, right this minute."

"... And?"

"And, the cause of death was strangulation with asphyxiation."

"... Strangulation with asphyxiation, by what means?"

"He was found hanging in his garage. There was a length of rope tied to a rafter. He was hanging by the neck from that rope."

"So, it was a suicide?"

Tony was quiet again. Sometimes he still struggles with how much he can tell me and what he should withhold. He cleared his throat before he spoke.

"This department will be conducting an investigation of a possible homicide."

"Ok, why?"

"You do know what I just told you is known to no one outside this department?"

"Yeah, I get it. I understand, you're the detective Lieutenant of the Robbery/Homicide division. Come on Tony, I'm not a reporter. There's a tie-in to a case I'm working on."

"What a surprise." He said.

"So, there is some sort of evidence leading you to suspect foul play?"

"Of course, Sherlock. What a brilliant deduction. However did you work it out?"

"Clues, Inspector Clouseau, it's all about the clues."

"So, I've heard." He growled.

CHAPTER 20

I had just gotten off the phone with Tony, when Jack called.

"Can you meet me in thirty minutes, in the same place we met last time?" There wasn't a real sense of urgency. He asked the question as though he were inviting me to have a cup of coffee.

"No, I have an appointment at Olympic Plaza. I'll meet you for lunch though."

"OK, when and where?"

"Let's say noon, at 'Currents'. Do you know where that is?"

"I'll figure it out."

"OK, see you then."

The whole conversation had been a subterfuge. He set the time. I verified the location. The bit about lunch at Currents was a red herring. There was always a possibility someone could be listening in. In this case it was pretty much a certainty. It was all I could do to avoid giving a big, warm Texas 'howdy' to the NSA or whoever Jack had monitoring my phone calls.

I would keep the meeting with Jack in thirty minutes at Olympic Plaza.

When I arrived at Olympic Plaza, Jack was already parked on the roof of the parking garage. He met me on foot, as I stepped out of my truck.

"Let's walk around and enjoy the view." He suggested.

Jack's suggestions are always just thinly veiled orders. This time I was not annoyed. It was a beautiful fall day in East Texas. A cold front had blown through, lowering the temperature to a more autumnal normal level. The sun was shining, but even up here on the roof of the parking garage the temperature was only about eighty degrees. I was already enjoying the breeze. The view out over the city was that of a dense green forest, with only the tallest buildings rising above it. The trees wouldn't begin to change color till the end of October.

As we walked, we were both constantly looking for observers or eavesdroppers. We saw only a few people coming or going from the medical complex. The top of the garage was reserved for docs and other employees but not many needed, and fewer wanted, to drive all the way up onto the roof. We were virtually alone up there.

"I understand you spent a couple of hours in the room of a visiting Mossad agent, last night." Jack informed me.

"No, it must have been some other guy your agents were following." I said. "Did you listen in on our conversation as well?"

"Now, John, don't go getting all bent out of shape. I have to keep tabs on everyone involved in this situation. No, I wasn't able to listen in on your... interactions, with the Mossad agent. I expect you to bring me up to speed, now. It's just part of the job. You remember how that works, right?"

"Yeah, I remember."

"Good. Now, what is the latest development?"

"We had a really great lead. Hakim, using the name Nat Baha, bought an electric guitar from a local pawnshop, three days ago. He was looking for some additional equipment. We were going to provide it and lure him to the pawnshop. Our plan to pick him up at the pawnshop fell through, because he had already found the equipment."

"So, he really is a musician. Damn! That was a good lead. What about Hafsah, did she have any luck with Aaron Parviz?"

"You tell me. Clearly, you know she met him."

"Stop being so petulant, of course we have Parviz under surveillance. I recognized Hafsah from the photos our agents took at the convenience store yesterday. No one knows who she is, but me. Her hijab was covering most of her face."

"I'm not being petulant. I just like my privacy. It used to be a right. Now privacy is more like a memory. There isn't anywhere you can go in any town where you aren't being photographed at some point, by someone. You never know who's watching you. I know you have somebody watching my every move, probably listening in on all my phone conversations as well. I don't like it."

"Paranoid much?" He asked.

"Even if I am paranoid, it doesn't mean federal agents aren't watching me."

"That's what they all say. Besides, if we are, it's a matter of national security," Jack reminded me, with the usual lack of emotion.

"In this case, yes. I accept that. But, when will it end?"

"Not until we've eliminated the threat. Did Hafsah make any progress with Parviz?"

I considered my response.

"Yes, she did. He's taken an intensely keen interest in her. We plan to leverage it. You should also know that Nat Baha has contacted some of the local recording studios. He's shopping prices, but I don't think he can afford to cut a demo record himself. I think he has other plans."

"I don't care about his recording plans. Do you have any idea what target they have in mind?"

"Not yet. If you have people watching the other

suspects, they should be able to determine if and when they start doing target assessment."

"Locally, they've attended movies, gone to sporting events and shopped at the mall. They've all done pretty much the same things, at a whole host of places in Dallas. Dallas is a much more target rich environment. The AT&T stadium alone holds tens of thousands of people. They may have already chosen the first target."

"Yes, I imagine they have." I agreed.

"But, you have no idea?"

"There's a big concert coming up in Tyler. Be a lot of people there for that."

"Which one, are you referring to the Tyler Symphony, Slippery G the rapper, or the Kyle Coltrane concert?" Jack asked.

"You've done your homework."

"Eternal vigilance is the price of freedom."

"Now you tell me."

"So, which one were you referring to?"

"Aaron Parviz will be playing drums with his band the Honky Tonk Broncs, as the opening act for Kyle Coltrane." I informed him.

"That's something to consider."

"I imagine you already have. I figure since you have people watching Parviz, you already knew about the concert and you have that angle covered."

"I've arranged to have the venue swept for explosives. You know, when a jihadist decides it's time to go to paradise, they kill as many infidels as they can in the process."

I was watching Jack carefully. He was avoiding eye contact with me. He was playing me in some way. It was as if he were talking in generalities, trying to skirt the real issue.

"I don't see that as being particularly likely. I don't think they're planning to go out with a big bang. You told me you thought this group planned to hit several targets in succession. Shoot up one place and move on to another, spreading as much terror around as they can, for as long as they can, before they get caught or killed."

"I still think so. I don't believe this group wants to go out in a single event. We believe they're planning to attack random and diverse public venues, like restaurants, sporting events, movie theaters and shopping malls. There's intelligence suggesting they're the first of several cells planning for a bigger offensive, randomly killing people without any apparent warning or provocation in several different towns and cities all over the country. It's not even a real network. The Islamic State has compartmented each cell, communicating with them independently. Other than Nat Baha, these are all self-radicalized American citizens. They want to make their fellow citizens afraid to go to any place where people are gathered. Their goal is to terrorize the populace so much; they effectively shut down our economy."

"It's barbaric and primitive. In this digital age, far more economic damage could be done through cyber warfare. Attacking and killing people as a means of geopolitical economic manipulation is a crude step backward in time.

Jack shook his head.

"At present, these jihadists don't have the sophistication, the capability, or the resources for effective cyber warfare. They have to rely on tried and true terror techniques. They seem bent on turning the world back about fourteen hundred years. Human beings are readily available and completely disposable to them. They'll do more than enough damage to our society by killing people at random."

"You don't think the Kyle Coltrane concert will be the big debut? It looks like most of the other suspects are going to be at that concert."

"How would I know?"

"The price of freedom is eternal vigilance." I said.

Jack nodded.

"So, I've heard."

CHAPTER 21

Christine came up with another idea. I was standing in the reception area, in front of Christine's desk.

"John, think about this. If Nat Baha is really a hot guitar man, he'll want several guitars. I could contact the local pawn shops and music stores again and dangle a worm. What if we had one of Stevie Ray Vaughan's guitars for sale? Most axe men would crawl across cut glass for one of those. You know how those guys are."

Actually, I wasn't even sure I understood what she had just said.

"Which guys?"

"Musicians, you know… electric guitar players."

"I don't think I understand you. Are you saying you can get a guitar that was played by Stevie Ray Vaughan?"

"No… Well, maybe. The point is we can say we have it, and … No, it won't work. We'd have to actually have the guitar, show pictures of it, and someone would have to be able to document that it was, in fact, one of Stevie's guitars. It would take too much time." Christine was chewing her lower lip. "Did you just roll your eyes?" she snapped at me.

I chuckled. "I'm sorry. I do understand your thinking, Christine. If we could come up with the right enticement, we could lure him out in the open."

"Exactly."

"What about an audition? Could we find a way to create a fake audition? I'm already fronting as a music producer looking for new talent?"

"Brilliant! That's it, John! I'll get started on it right away. We could rent a local recording studio for a day or two. It'll be expensive though."

"Set it up. Our client can afford it.

"Honestly, John, you surprise me sometimes."

"God's mercies are new every morning."

Christine smiled at me.

"Yes, they certainly are. Speaking of which, what is Hafsah doing today?"

I knew Hafsah was attempting to make contact with a man by the name of Abdul Suliman. He was another of the suspects included in the file Jack had given me. Mr. Suliman owned a machine shop. Hafsah was going to approach him pretending to be an interior designer. She would ask him if he would be able to convert several large ceramic vases and some oddly shaped copper vessels into table lamps. In the process, she hoped to have a look at his shop and whoever might be there.

I also knew Christine didn't want to know about these things.

"What does Ms. Bashir have to do with God's mercies?" I asked her.

"If sending that woman into your life is not an example of God's mercy…"

I saw the humor in her comment, but I also saw the truth of it. I was stunned.

"I think Hafsah was planning to do some shopping today." I said, as I headed for my office. "Let me know how the audition idea progresses."

Christine wasn't having it. She followed me into my office.

"John, I'm sorry. I was just kidding. I didn't mean to hurt your feelings."

I sat down at my desk.

"You didn't hurt my feelings, Christine. You actually just helped me realize how true your statement is."

"Don't be ridiculous. You're a good looking, eligible bachelor. Any single lady would be proud to have you taking an interest in her. Remember, I've seen women practically throwing themselves at you."

There was so much Christine didn't know about me. She didn't know my service on earth as a Shepherd had made it... impractical, for me to have a wife and family. My appointment as an ambassador of heaven had provided me with certain special gifts and abilities, but my mission had also prevented me from experiencing some of the comforts and joys ordinary men might appreciate.

Now things had changed. I was certain God had sent Hafsah in to my life. What did this mean? Why now, after all these years? Did this mean an end to my mission on earth? If not, was I completely wrong in my attraction and emotional response to Hafsah? Had I succumbed to the weakness of the flesh, and been overwhelmed by earthly temptation?

Maybe I was over analyzing the situation. One thing was clear. I had never been so unsure of what I should do at any time in all the decades since I had become a Shepherd.

I was shaken by this revelation.

"Sometime, I'll discuss the matter with you in more detail. Don't worry I saw the humor in your comment. Right now, I'm OK. I just have a lot on my mind. I need to be working."

"You're sure?" Christine asked.

"I'm sure about that, some other things, not so much."

"Is there any part of it you can talk to me about?"

I took a long slow breath. I would have to tell her something. Could I tell her that because of the life I've chosen, everyone I've ever loved is dead and everyone I will ever love will probably die before I do? No, not yet.

"I guess I've just been single for so long, it's hard to imagine having a woman in my life."

"So, what am I, chopped liver?"

I laughed.

"Hardly, but you know what I mean."

She smiled.

"Are you so committed to the bachelor life, you can't imagine something better?"

I considered the question. It required a careful answer. What was wrong with me? Why were my emotions getting the best of me?

"No, it's not that. On the contrary, I can imagine having Hafsah in my life. Up until now, I've only imagined what it might be like. Will you run along and let me get some work done?"

CHAPTER 22

"I'm in love with her, John." Tony said.

We were having lunch together at Currents restaurant. It was kind of a posh place. Probably a little too frou-frou for a couple of working stiffs like Tony and me, but I figured since somebody would be expecting me to be there, I might as well show up. I hate to eat alone.

I had mentioned something about Christine in the course of our typically sophisticated and erudite conversation, and Tony just blurted it out.

"Yeah, Tony, I'm aware of that. I expect she feels the same way about you."

"No, John, what I'm saying is; I can't imagine my life without her. I'm going to ask her to marry me."

I was amused by his intensity and his candor. I had known Tony for several years. I had been there for him when he lost his wife and son in a highway accident. He struggled through the loss, but he had been sustained by his faith, with a little help from me. He had been rattling around all alone in his big, empty three-bedroom house for too long"

"Really, Tony? That's terrific."

"Is it? I mean, do you think she'll say 'yes'?"

"I expect so, but you'll never know till you pop the question."

"Yeah…" He was lost in thought for a moment. Then he looked at me.

"You'll be my best man, right?"

"Of course, I will. I'm honored. Thank you for asking."

He nodded his answer.

"I guess we'll have to get married in Kerrville, where her folks live." He mused.

I chuckled.

"Kind of putting the cart before the horse, don't you think?"

"Huh? Oh, yeah. I think I have a good way to ask her."

"On bended knee?"

"Probably, but I want it to be a surprise and something she'll never forget."

"Tony, I promise you, once you ask Christine to marry you, she'll never forget it."

"Oh, sure, but I want it to be special."

The waiter came and gathered up our empty plates.

I shrugged and said, "I've been under the impression asking that question tends to be very special for most women."

"Sure, but… I have an idea."

"What is it?"

"I can't tell you, yet. I'm not sure I can pull it off. In the meantime, you can't say a word to Christine about this. OK?" Tony was very earnest.

"Your secret is safe with me." I grinned. "Now tell me a little bit more about this dead guitar player. What makes you think it might've been a homicide?"

Tony took a moment to think about what he was willing to divulge. The waiter came back and asked if we wanted coffee. We did.

When the waiter had brought us our coffee, Tony spoke up.

"His name was Jeff Tolbert. His girlfriend and his family agree that he wasn't depressed or in any way suicidal. In fact they say he was all jacked up, excited about the upcoming concert."

"That's insufficient reason to open a homicide investigation."

"The evidence at the scene was inconclusive."

"What's inconclusive about finding someone hanging from a rafter?" I asked.

"It's not what we found; it's what we didn't find."

"No note?"

"You're jumping to conclusions, Poirot."

I chuckled, ducking my head to concede the point.

Tony went on. "He did leave a note, sort of. It was posted on Facebook. The usual sort of thing, you know. 'I hate myself, there's no hope, I just can't take it anymore,' like that."

I nodded slowly, waiting for the other shoe to drop.

When Tony didn't say anything, I prompted him.

"So, what was missing?"

"His girlfriend found him hanging in the shed they used as a garage. She couldn't untie the knot, because the rope went over the rafter and was tied to one of the wall posts. His weight made the knot too tight."

I was wondering where he was going with this.

"She called 911, and then she ran back to the house and got a kitchen knife. She used it to cut the rope. When the emergency people arrived on the scene, they found him already deceased, lying exactly where he fell when she cut the rope."

Tony began swirling the last of his coffee in the bottom of his cup.

"Am I missing something here?" I was getting annoyed.

"That was my thought. There was something that bothered me about the crime scene. Something I was missing. Then it dawned on me. She found him hanging in the middle of the empty garage, nearly two feet in the air. Then I knew what was missing."

I waited for it.

"There was no knocked over stool or ladder. Nothing he could've climbed up on. There was a lawnmower stored over in a corner, too far away for him to have used, and it was too low to the ground. How did he get up there?"

"Good question." I said.

"His girlfriend is barely five feet tall and slight. She didn't lift him up there."

"If she didn't kill him, would she have helped him commit suicide?"

"Nope. She was in town when it happened. No way she had anything to do with it. Another thing, there were rope burns on the insides of his hands."

"Do you think he could've jumped up, grabbed the noose and slipped it over his own neck?"

"I considered that, until the coroner told me there were some faint ligature marks on his wrists."

"As though his hands had been tied behind his back?"

Tony nodded his affirmative.

"A more thorough examination of the rafter and the rope showed clear evidence of abrasion. Somebody put the rope around his neck, tossed the rope over the rafter, and hauled him off his feet, maybe three feet in the air. They tied the rope to the post, untied his hands, and left him there, kicking, as he strangled to death. He had managed to get a hold of the rope, but he couldn't lift himself high enough, long enough. Then, his hands slipped."

After a moment, I asked the obvious question. "Any idea who might've done it?"

Tony sighed.

"Not at this time."

CHAPTER 23

As the sound of the chimes died away, I heard some-one approaching the front door. It was opened by the grief-stricken lady of the house, Rosie Ferguson's mother, her face drawn and pale.

"Hello, Mrs. Ferguson. May I come in?"

She lowered her eyes and nodded, stepping aside to let me pass.

"Who is it, Joan?" Mr. Ferguson called, from another room.

Closing the door, Mrs. Ferguson didn't reply. She looked at me and gestured toward the living room.

Inside, I waited for Mrs. Ferguson to have a seat on the sofa.

I turned as Mr. Ferguson came into the room.

"Tucker, what are you doing here? We have no fur-ther need of your services. Didn't you get the check I sent you?" Mr. Ferguson scowled at me as he spoke.

"Yes, I did. Thank you. I just wanted to stop by and tell you both how sorry I am for your loss. Fol-lowing a lead, I asked Lieutenant Escalante to meet me at the place where we found your daughter and her boyfriend."

"He wasn't her boyfriend." Mr. Ferguson's yelled. His complexion was approaching a color I would call "scarlet indignation" or perhaps "ruby wrath".

"You were there? You found Rosie?" Mrs. Ferguson asked.

"Yes, ma'am. A witness told me they had seen a green Chevy truck at that location. I'm so sorry. I got there too late to save Rosie and Jeff."

"You couldn't have saved them. Nobody could." Mr. Ferguson scoffed.

"Why do you say that? If I had learned where they were only a day earlier, they'd still be alive."

"Their fate was sealed the moment they ran off."

"What are you saying? You told me, you believed Jeff abducted Rosie."

"Whatever. I want you to leave. Get the hell out of here."

Ignoring her husband's growing rage, Mrs. Ferguson said, "Please have a seat, Mr. Tucker. You'll excuse me if I don't offer any refreshment."

"Yes, ma'am. Thank you." I chose a wingback chair opposite the sofa. I avoided eye contact with Mr. Ferguson."

"Is there anything you can tell me about... I mean... was it..." Mrs. Ferguson struggled to form her question.

"Rosie and Jimmy were camped in a spot about seven miles north of here. They had shelter and supplies. So, they were as comfortable as could be expected."

"You call that camping? That rusty old building is nasty, squalid and vermin infested. No place for my girl." Mr. Ferguson said.

"By all appearances they were happy there — happy being there, together."

Mr. Ferguson staggered forward. "No. That's a lie, Rosie could never be happy with anyone but me."

I suspected his blood pressure was approaching something akin to explosive decompression.

"Did my daughter suffer, Mr. Tucker?" Mrs. Ferguson asked.

How do you answer a question like that? What definition of suffering would apply in this case?

"No ma'am. She was killed instantly. Wouldn't you agree, Mr. Ferguson?"

He nodded and said, "I think so."

That told me all I needed to know. I stood up.

Turning to face Mr. Ferguson, I said, "I think she probably suffered more when she was living in this house."

Mrs. Ferguson cried out and broke down, violent spasms shaking her as she sobbed into her hands.

"You son of a bitch," Mr. Ferguson snarled, lunging for me.

Anticipating his attack, I blocked his outstretched arms with my left forearm and slammed the heel of my right hand just below his left ear. His forward momentum combined with my blow sent him crashing into the coffee table, which shattered and collapsed under him.

The front door burst open, and three uniformed police officers in tactical gear ran into the room. Two of them jumped on Mr. Ferguson, pinning him to the floor as he struggled to get free.

Tony walked in behind the officers. "Robert Joseph Ferguson, you are under arrest for the murders of James Duncan and Rosemarie Ferguson. If you continue to struggle, Officer Miller will taze you. That failing, if you continue to resist arrest, one or all of us will shoot you. You have the right to try. Go ahead, try."

All the fight went out of Ferguson. The officers cuffed him, hauled him to his feet and read him his rights.

He stood with his head hanging down, looking only at the floor. Officers were holding his arms, one on each side.

"Did you get it all, Tony?" I asked.

"Yes, J. W. Loud and clear. I figure with the recording, the forensics, your testimony, Priscilla's — this guy's going away for the rest of his life. Too easy if you ask me."

I stepped in front of Bob Ferguson. "Mr. Ferguson, look at me. When you get where you're going, I hope you'll pay attention to the prison chaplain. No matter what you've done, there's help and healing, forgiveness, and restoration for you if you repent and ask God. No sin is too great, nor any man too vile, for the grace of God. Do you understand what I'm saying?"

He stared right through me, as though at an on-coming locomotive, looking into the face of some horror in a place the rest of us couldn't see.

Tony pointed at the open door. "Get him outta here, boys."

Mrs. Ferguson continued sobbing. I walked into the kitchen and returned with a dish towel I had soaked in cold tap water and wrung out. Sitting beside her I pulled her hands away from her face and began gently wiping away her tears. She leaned back on the cushions and let me bathe her face.

Tony sat on the sofa typing a text message on his phone.

When her breathing returned to normal and she was calmer, I said, "Thank you, Mrs. Ferguson. We know this was nearly more than you could bear. You were very brave."

"All these years, how could I let him… That monster."

"You have to learn to forgive yourself. The situation developed without your knowledge. By the time you found out, it was beyond your ability to confront. You feared what he might do."

"I failed my daughter and got her killed." Hot tears were again streaming down her face.

"The first step toward healing is acknowledging your brokenness. You didn't have anything to do with her death. That was all his doing. You can't go back and change what happened, but you can go forward into new life."

"Can I?"

"Yes, ma'am, I promise. Here's the number of a friend of mine. She's a psychologist and a gifted counselor." I handed her the card. "She'll help you work your way through this. It'll take some time…"

I was interrupted by the chimes of the doorbell.

Tony answered the door. When he returned, he wasn't alone.

Priscilla Davidson and her mother were with him.

Those ladies took charge of Joan Ferguson and wrapped her up in their loving care, telling her how much God loved her and that they were there for her.

Tony and I took the opportunity to make excuses and let ourselves out.

CHAPTER 24

It was just a matter of time, Hafsah was thinking. Time, it wasn't as linear as most people thought. Time was not just a ticking clock, the turning of the earth, or one thing leading to another. Many things occurred simultaneously. At times she sensed a fire and passion in the man threatening to consume her. She was drawn to him, as a moth to a flame. Other times, he seemed distant and uninterested in her or even in the hunt for Nat Baha. He would drift away as though he were thinking about something else.

Why was he so reluctant to do what had to be done? Was he incapable of wrapping his head around the fact there was no other option, except to kill Baha?

It was the same with their growing attraction to each other. She had finally stopped trying to deny it. There it was, she wanted to be with him. He was clearly attracted to her, she was certain of it. She sensed within him a struggle. What was it?

Often, when they were together, he would throw up walls and withdraw. What had happened in his life to make him so reserved? Perhaps it was the importance of the mission. Maybe he was still trying to maintain some sort of professional distance. No, they had already crossed that line. It was as if he was afraid to get too close to her. Who had hurt him so badly he was nearly crippled by it?

On the other hand, maybe it was for the best. Perhaps he was saving her from herself. What was she thinking? This was a mission. She had no time for romance. Until now she had always been able to avoid the complications of intimate relationships. She was on the move, at large and in charge. What was wrong with her?

There were moments with John when she was as giddy as a schoolgirl. Images of wedding gowns and children's names danced just outside her consciousness. But that was all there could be – dreams. She would be moving on soon, when Baha was dead. Her entire focus needed to be on killing her cousin.

John was right about choosing the time and place. They couldn't afford to attempt killing Baha when he was anywhere near innocent citizens. In a bid to escape, he'd kill anyone and everyone around him. If they could lead him into a trap, the matter could be more safely brought to a close. This plan of luring him to a recording studio might just work.

Now, she was no longer following in the wake of her cousin's murders. Finally, she was ahead of him. Her cousin might not be able to resist the opportunity to make a recording of his music. It was the one hope they had, and the opportunity was only three days distant.

It was just a matter of time. Three days. She sensed they were running out of time. Every heart beat reminded her of the ticking clock.

She was convinced Baha was very near. These locals knew where he was. Everything pointed to it. In most other countries, she and her team would've taken one of these men and made him talk. Here in America it was more problematic. It wasn't easy to snatch someone off the streets. They couldn't have the police involved. Of course, John would never permit it – if he knew of the plan. They also ran the risk of tipping off her cousin. If he thought his mission was in jeopardy, he would simply disappear, again.

It was just a matter of time. Three days. In three days, this would all be over. She would be leaving this place, and leaving John behind. Could she?

Did she imagine she could stay here with this man? Could she really settle down in a small city in East Texas, and become a – what was the term – soccer mom? Ridiculous!

Would John go away with her? How would that work? No, that too was ridiculous.

What was wrong with her? Why couldn't she shake these feelings? And, what was his problem? Why didn't he come right out and say what he wanted and expected from the relationship?

No. it was for the best, she'd be leaving. She didn't need to make any foolish mistakes. But, before then, she wanted desperately to break through his barriers and get to know him better.

It was just a matter of time.

CHAPTER 25

My phone rang. The caller ID showed it was Hafsah, so I answered it.

"This is, John…"

"Hello, John. I was thinking we might have a picnic this evening. Are you free?"

"Hi. Yes, I think I can get free, pretty much any-time you like. How did your shopping go today?"

"I think I may have found the things I needed."

"Well, that's nice. What time would you like me to pick you up?"

"Would four thirty be a feasible time? I thought you might know a suitable place where we could have our picnic and watch the sunset."

"I'll think of somewhere. What would you like me to bring?"

"I should have everything we will need. Just come pick me up at the hotel."

I found Hafsah waiting for me in the lobby of her hotel. Today, she was dressed in blue and grey 'urban camouflage' pants, black hiking boots and a dark grey long-sleeved t-shirt (which accentuated her curves), under a light-weight, navy blue jacket. Her dark hair was again pulled back into a pony tail.

The whole affect was feminine, casual and practical, suitable for either a hike in the woods or hiding in a dark alley. Her attire was a perfect complement to my blue jeans and long-sleeved black shirt, under a charcoal grey field jacket and a black ball cap. She had an old-fashioned picnic basket with a red and white checked table cloth folded on top under the handles.

"Wow, Hafsah, I'm impressed. I haven't seen a picnic basket like that in years. I can't imagine how challenging it must've been for your logistics and supply people to come up with one."

She looked at me innocently and said.

"Whatever do you mean, John? I told you I had been out shopping."

For just a second, I was confused. I had been certain our previous phone conversation was about something else entirely."

"Gotcha!" she said, grinning.

I made a face.

"Do you mind if we take a different vehicle? I have use of a friend's SUV. Perhaps it would be more suitable to our adventure?" Hafsah asked.

"Hmmm. You really have been shopping."

She smiled and handed me the keys.

The SUV turned out to be a brand-new Chevy Tahoe. The Tahoe was black as midnight, but shiny with the show-room clear-coat and sparkling with chrome. We drove out of the parking lot turning right onto Grande. I was planning to turn left onto Broadway, thinking I would head on out to Lake Palestine for our picnic.

"John, we're going to go north on Broadway. You'll need to get in the right lane."

I glanced over at her. Her face was all business.

"OK. Do you want to tell me where we're going?"

"We are going back to the machine shop that is owned by Mr. Suliman, on the north side of the town."

"Rats." I responded.

"What? Where do you see rats?" She asked, looking around and sounding almost alarmed.

"No rats. It's just an expression suggesting disappointment."

She smiled. "Oh, yes of course."

"Why are we going to the machine shop? What did you find there?"

She looked over at me as I turned onto Broadway.

"Well, Mr. Tucker, I think I may have found Nat Baha."

Twenty minutes later, we were heading north on Broadway toward where it became Farm to Market road 14. As we approached the intersection with Loop 323, Hafsah pointed across the loop.

"That is Mr. Suliman's machine shop over there," she said.

We had to stop for the red light and it gave us a moment to study the rusting steel buildings in the light of the early evening sun. The place appeared to be deserted, the rolling, eight-foot-tall, steel mesh gate was closed and secured by a heavy chain and padlock. The fully paved lot and small complex of interconnected buildings was completely surrounded by an eight-foot-tall chain link fence, topped with concertina wire.

When the traffic light changed, we crossed the loop and studied the buildings as we drove past. There were no vehicles parked where we could see them. In the gloom of late afternoon, the place had the kind of run-down look only old industrial settings can achieve. There was a scattering of the common detritus of unidentifiable trash, plastic buckets, rusting metal and old wooden pallets leaning against the buildings.

"Keep going north," Hafsah instructed me.

"OK, but there isn't much up this way till we get to the interstate," I observed.

"We are going farther, all the way to the Tyler State Park."

"The State Park, really? Why there?"

"We will have our picnic," Hafsah said with a smile. "Then we will come back here and we will search the machine shop."

"Why? Do you think Nat Baha may be hiding there?"

"Mr. Suliman was happy to show me his machine shop. He has a variety of heavy machinery for fabrication and welding, as well as the usual assortment of smaller hand and power tools. He only employs two or three workmen. In one building I saw a work table with some odds and ends of tools and bits of metal on it. He did not pay any attention to that table, but I did."

I looked at Hafsah, indicating my interest in her story.

"I showed no obvious interest in the table, because what was on the table, partly covered by a shop towel, were three receivers for Kalashnikov assault rifles. AK 47s, to be more precise. There were no barrels, stocks, magazines, or anything else in evidence that would have been apparent to most people. I believe those receivers were being modified from semi-automatic firing capability, to fully automatic capability. That would be illegal in your country, would it not?"

"It's possible to get a federal permit, but I doubt a local machine shop would be permitted to modify AKs. Still, that alone doesn't indicate Nat Baha might be hiding there."

"I also saw an electronic amplifier, huge speakers, an electric guitar, a stool, some cables and some other things over in a corner of one of the buildings. I asked about these things, because it was clearly incongruous in a machine shop."

I nodded, "Yeah, it is interesting."

"Mr. Suliman told me those were his nephew's musical instruments and that his nephew would sometimes practice out there. He then dragged a tarpaulin over and covered the equipment."

"Sounds reasonable," I observed, as I turned in to the park entrance.

"Of course, it sounds reasonable, but there are too many coincidences. I do not believe in coincidence, John."

I looked over at her and said, "I knew we had something in common."

CHAPTER 26

The sun was just setting as we spread the table cloth out over a picnic table. From this spot, we had a lovely view of the lake. She opened the picnic basket and pulled out plates, napkins, and cutlery, even some plastic wine glasses. Then, Hafsah brought forth a bottle of Argentine Malbec, a spiced cheese, sourdough bread and some fried chicken!

She saw the startled look on my face.

"What were you expecting I would have brought for a picnic dinner? Have I forgotten something? " She asked, clearly concerned.

"No, Hafsah, I couldn't be more pleased. This looks fantastic. I guess I thought the picnic basket was a prop, you had hidden weapons in there, or something like that."

"Prop? Do you mean faux, like a theater dressing?"

"The thought crossed my mind."

"Maybe you were expecting me to pull out an Uzi, or a dagger?"

"Well, a dagger would be useful for slicing the bread."

"… Or slicing your throat. You cannot just pull the bread apart?" She growled.

"Oh, yes of course… I uhh… I only meant…"

Hafsah laughed. "Gotcha, again! Honestly John, you make it very easy for me to have sport with you."

"I aim to please." I chuckled.

"It is beautiful, is it not?" Hafsah asked, looking around at the pine forest and the lake, with the setting sun reflected on its surface in shades of gold, orange, red and purple.

I only had eyes for her. "Yes, beautiful." I said.

She caught me looking and she blushed a little. Maybe it was just the coloring of the sunset.

We sat and ate and laughed as the sun went down.

It was fully dark as we put the remains of our picnic back in the SUV. Hafsah opened the back hatch of the Tahoe and the interior lights revealed a black duffle bag on the floor.

She turned to me. "In that bag you will find tools and weapons. Also there is night vision gear. We will go now to the machine shop. I will show you where to park. We must be stealthy. I saw no alarms, but Hakim is clever and he will be alert for trouble. Are you any good at close quarters, hand to hand combat?"

"I was a SEAL, Hafsah. I have the best training Uncle Sam can provide, but I've also spent some time with the Palmach, and I honed my close combat skills with Ini Lichtenfeld." I said.

"I read something about that in your dossier. How is it possible? I think Lichtenfeld died about twenty years ago." Hafsah observed.

"What I mean is I studied Krav Maga with one of his students."

"You say you spent time with the Palmach. Wasn't the Palmach part of Haganah? Haganah became the Israeli Defense Force more than sixty years ago. I don't think anyone who was in either Palmach or Haganah is still living."

"Not many, no. I must say, you have a surprising understanding of Israeli history."

"But you said…"

"It's not important. The point is I can take care of myself. What about you? You can't weigh more than a hundred and ten pounds, soaking wet. I don't think hand to hand combat would be recommended for you."

Hafsah ignored my comment and unzipped the bag. She started to hand me a Glock nine millimeter, but I declined it.

"I've got a .45 tucked behind my back."

"Do you have a sound suppressor for it?" She asked.

"No, but I'm not planning to use it, anyway."

Hafsah slapped me, very fast and very hard. I never saw it coming.

"Wake up! This man will kill you. I cannot take you with me if you do not have your mind on the mission. Take this Glock and this suppressor. Do you know how to attach it?"

"Yes, of course." I was thinking how suddenly Hafsah had gone from being the soft, sweet woman I had been kissing only moments before, into this hardened, combat ready... hellcat.

"Are you with me in this?" She asked, sharply.

"Hoo-ah." I growled, by way of reply.

Hafsah put her face close to mine. She looked deeply into my eyes.

"I am sorry, John. There is a time and place for everything. Now is the time to prepare to make war, not love. Now is the time to think about how to stay alive. If you cannot do this..."

"It's done! What else do you have in the bag?"

Hafsah smiled sadly. She pulled out another Glock in a black shoulder holster with two extra magazines on the off-side. She shed her jacket and shrugged into the shoulder rig. As she put her jacket back on, she pointed at the bag.

"There are two Uzis, also with sound suppressors, extra magazines for the Uzis and our handguns, night vision gear and tools to breach the fence and the padlocks. You will also find grenades and most anything else we might need. We will leave our identification in the vehicle, to be retrieved later. You will take your orders from me and do exactly as I instruct you. Is this understood?"

I was tempted to ask her if there were sound suppressors on the grenades. It was exactly the type of question we would have asked back in the SEALs, but I could tell explosives humor was not her style.

"Yes ma'am." I answered, firmly. I didn't even smile, at least not so she could see it.

"Do you have any questions before we begin this operation?"

"Did you see an alarm system or surveillance cameras?"

She nodded. "There are three cameras. There is a surveillance camera pointed at the front gate, one pointed at the parking lot and one directed down over the front door. I saw no cameras inside the building. There is no apparent alarm system, but there could be motion detectors."

"I doubt it. Considering the location and the conditions, that machine shop is unlikely to employ anything so sophisticated. What about cameras at the other doors?"

"I did not observe any as we drove past the buildings. I'm confident the other doors were without cameras." She replied.

"Where are your Mossad teammates?"

"They will be close by, securing our vehicle and ready to provide emergency reinforcement, transportation, diversionary activity, or whatever other assistance we require."

"How will we communicate with each other?"

"You and I will be close together at all times. We will use hand signals as necessary. Are there any other questions?"

"Yes, Hafsah. Will you pray with me?"

Hafsah blinked several times, and then she slowly nodded her head.

"Yes, John, I will pray with you."

I took both her hands in mine and closed my eyes. I thanked God for His grace and mercy, for His provision in all things. I thanked Him for bringing Hafsah into my life and for guidance in the thing we were about to do. I waited a moment to hear if Hafsah might have something to say. She didn't. I prayed that Hafsah might come to know His son, our savior. I closed by saying "Come quickly, Lord Jesus."

When I opened my eyes, I found Hafsah staring at me.

"You speak to God as though you know him, as though you felt his presence, as though you were talking to a much-loved father. Is this not so?"

"Yes, it is so." I smiled at her.

"You speak of Jesus as though he were still alive..."

"He is alive, Hafsah. He is no longer here on earth, because He completed His mission here. Because of what He did, I live. Because of what He did, I can call God 'Abba' - father. The God of creation looks upon me as one of His children whom He loves.

"You can call God 'Abba'? That is an intimate term, like you are saying 'daddy'." She said, marveling.

I nodded, with a smile.

Hafsah choked a little, and said. "All this week, I have seen Jesus in my dreams. As a child I was taught that Jesus was an important prophet, not as important as Mohammad, but a prophet all the same. I do not dream about Mohammad, but sometimes when I dream, Jesus holds me tenderly in his arms. When he holds me, I feel clean and safe and... loved. Then I wake up to this horrible world, the comfort quickly fades and I am left with only the vague memory of the dream."

"I told you, Jesus is alive. Would you like to meet Him?"

For a moment Hafsah looked startled. I sensed her struggling. Then her features changed again.

"Yes, but not tonight. Tonight, we will kill Hakim." Hafsah had regained her hardened countenance and determination. "It is time to go."

CHAPTER 27

Following Hafsah's directions, I pulled off the road on a dirt driveway that ended in a partially fenced vacant lot. It hadn't been mowed or maintained in quite some time. Our Tahoe was screened from the road by the saplings and brush that had grown up in it. There was a bank of trees down one side of the lot.

Hafsah had filled me in on the plan as we drove down from Tyler State Park.

After I parked the Tahoe under the trees in a spot well hidden from the road, we pulled the rucksack out of the rear compartment of the Tahoe and fished out the night vision gear and a couple of black balaclavas. We pulled on the balaclavas leaving only our eyes uncovered. Once we had the night vision gear on, our faces were completely hidden.

"Once we get on the other side of these trees, we will be on the north side of the machine shop. This is the backside of the property and completely hidden from sight of anyone driving by. We will come up against the chain link fence. Once we get there, we must remain silent. Remember what I said. We stick together and you follow my lead." She had that kind of green and hazy look everything gets in the enhanced ambient light as seen through night vision optics.

"OK, lead on." I said, hefting the rucksack.

With two Uzis, extra magazines, tools and grenades, the bag was bulky and somewhat more heavy than practical, but I had been designated as the pack animal. Hafsah had commanded we be silent, so I refrained from braying.

We eased through about fifteen yards of brush and deadfall limbs under the trees almost as quietly as deer through the forest, although perhaps lacking the same grace.

Soon we were at the chain link fence, about midway on the north side of the machine shop. Everything inside the fence appeared to be paved or oily, hard-packed ground. The air was heavy with the smell of creosote, oil and burnt metal.

We took a moment to observe the back of the buildings. There was one security light burning, and it was mounted on an electric service pole at the front of the property on the edge of the parking lot. We were about eighteen feet from the back of the nearest building. From the edge of the fence to the back of the building there was an open-sided structure with a sloping steel roof. There were a couple of fifty gallon drums, some pallets and stacked steel plate, bar stock and pipe in various dimensions, stored here.

I looked at Hafsah, and her greenish, almost spectral image pointed at the fence and made a cutting motion with two fingers of a gloved hand, scissoring.

I opened the rucksack and pulled out the heavy bolt cutters. Hafsah put her hand over mine and indicated I should wait for a moment. She dug into the rucksack and came out with a smaller and lighter version. In five minutes, I had cut through the bottom of the eight-foot tall fence just high enough to allow our passage through. First Hafsah, then the rucksack and lastly, I eased through the fence.

Once we were on the property, we paused to reconnoiter. Hafsah pointed at me, then at herself, then at an easterly corner of the nearest building.

I nodded and followed her to the corner, carrying the rucksack. Hafsah took a quick look around the corner then looked back around for a more extended study. She took my hand and pulled as she went around the corner, ducked low. I followed right behind her, carrying the heavy duffle.

Half a dozen quick strides brought us to a loading dock. There were some stairs on the side of it. A big overhead door could be opened to allow shipping and receiving of heavy objects or truckloads of pretty much anything. There was a single, dirty light bulb in an old steel fixture above the overhead door. The door was latched into a fixture in the concrete with a padlock securing it. We went up the stairs and the heavy bolt cutter made light work of the padlock. As quietly as possible, we lifted the door, just high enough for both of us to duck under.

Inside, it was very dark. The only light was that which spilled in under the edge of the overhead door from the feeble light bulb outside, and whatever ambient light that could get through the few small, grimy windows mounted in the walls high above us. If we hadn't had the night vision gear, we would have been virtually blind.

Hafsah flipped a switch on the bracket of her night vision gear and the light in the room increased noticeably. I knew she had switched on a diffused red light that provided a small amount of additional illumination without being visible from outside the building. I switched mine on as well, and now we could clearly see all of the objects and structures within about ten feet of us. I could also see the Glock she now carried in her hand.

This was a shipping/receiving area accustomed to sporadic utility. The building was like a small abandoned warehouse, virtually empty. There were a couple of pallets leaning against a wall, another with a fifty-gallon drum of some sort of industrial lubricant sitting on it. The only other thing in the building our search revealed was something off in a corner, covered by a tarp. Under the tarp we found two big speakers, an amplifier, an electric guitar and a boom-box with a handful of CDs.

We looked over the musical equipment and I noticed the CDs were all techno rock, or head banger music.

Hafsah tapped me on the shoulder and indicated we should continue the search.

All of the buildings that made up the machine shop were interconnected. Some were separated by heavy sliding doors and others had overhead pulleys and conveyors for moving heavy objects from one building into the next. We went through the whole place, room by room, but found no secret hideout with Hakim lurking inside it. In one room, Hafsah led me to the workbench where apparently, she had seen the AK 47 receivers. They were gone, but I recognized the brass and steel objects left on the bench as typical gunsmith tools.

In all, it took us the better part of an hour and a half to do a slow, thorough, but fruitless search of the machine shop complex. We had managed to locate and grab the only computer in the place.

When we got back into the shipping/receiving room, I went to the musical equipment and started putting whatever would fit into the duffle bag. Hafsah appeared to be impatient and even tried to reject the electric guitar when I thrust it at her, but I was insistent so she complied. She had more trouble getting the guitar through the gap in the fence than I had with the now overstuffed duffle bag.

We didn't speak until we got back to where the Tahoe was parked.

As we pulled off our night vision gear, Hafsah snapped at me.

"Why did you make me drag this worthless guitar all the way back here?"

I grinned at her.

"It's just subterfuge, my dear. We stole the computer and the other electronic things that were easy to carry. Typical petty theft, they'll chock it up to the cost of doing business in this part of town.

"The whole exercise has proven to be a waste of time." Hafsah lamented.

"Not really, we know Nat Baha isn't here and apparently he's never been here."

"What about the guitar? She asked. "Don't you think it's a link to him?"

"No, I don't think it is. I think we'll find that Mr. Suliman really does have a nephew who plays his guitar in his mostly empty building."

"Why do you say that?"

"The equipment is cheap and the only music the guitar player was trying to emulate was thrash music, punk rock. I believe your cousin is much more sophisticated than that."

"How do you know this?"

"Call it a hunch." I said.

Hafsah sighed. "Yes, you are probably correct. I do not know anything about the heavy punk rock style of music."

"It's mostly about the message, which is usually screamed, rather than sung. Thrasher music in particular tends to be raw. There's often a dearth of sophistication and nuance in the music." I said.

While we had been ducking, crawling and crab walking through the dirty, greasy and debris filled buildings, trying not to get cut or stabbed by bits of sharp metal, I had come to a decision. It was time to tell Hafsah something she probably already suspected.

"Hafsah, there's something else you should know." I said, taking her arm.

"What is it, John?" She asked, alarmed.

"The United States Department of Homeland Security has Mr. Suliman under constant surveillance."

"John, how could you know... Oh, I see." Hafsah jerked her arm out of my hand.

"I wanted to tell you before now..."

"Tell me what, that you are a federal agent?" She asked coldly.

"No, I am not a federal agent. I told you the truth. I got the file from a guy in the DHS. He told me everyone in that folder is presently under suspicion and subject to surveillance. My point is, if Hakim were here, they would have known about it. I don't think they would overlook an opportunity to catch someone like him."

"Perhaps they would not, if they knew who he is, and if they are competent enough to catch him. Would they tell you if they did?"

"I think if they had anything solid on Suliman, Parviz, or any of them, they would have snatched them up in a heartbeat."

"So, why do you tell me this now?"

"I think we're wasting our time on these guys. Your cousin is hidden somewhere else. Let's leave these guys to the DHS and you and I stay focused on Nat Baha."

"But you must see that this was a good lead."

"It seemed like a good idea at the time, I didn't really have time to think it through. Besides, I was kind of looking forward to a moonlit picnic" I said.

Hafsah refused to be distracted from the topic at hand.

"Without researching each of these men, we have no idea where Hakim is, or how to find him." She observed.

"Remember, I have Christine working on an angle that might bring Hakim to us."

"Angle, do you mean like fishing? Yes, I see. We bait the line and hope he takes the hook," She said, with some enthusiasm.

"Well, not really... uh, OK. Sure, that's it exactly. Here's what we have in mind..."

CHAPTER 28

His band of fighters hadn't taken the supposed suicide death of one of their number without some reaction. Nat Baha quickly put a stop to any dissension.

"Understand my brothers, this is the example set for us by the Prophet himself – may he be forever revered and adored. We must strike the neck of anyone who betrays us. Jeff Tolbert was not a true Muslim, nor a true friend. He was an infidel who would have betrayed us and ruined everything we have committed ourselves to do. We must be willing to cut off our own hand if it would cause us to stray from our course. From this day forward, our cause is one; Death to the infidel, Allahu Akbar!"

"Death to the infidel. Allahu Akbar! Allahu Akbar! Allahu Akbar!" The men shouted in unison.

Nodding in satisfaction he went on.

"Thanks to Mr. Suliman, our weapons have all been converted to fully automatic capability. Each has been test-fired. He assures me we have enough ammunition for both the mission, and for practice drills. Who will volunteer first?"

Jahander Khalid raised his hand.

"Very well, Jahander my brother. You will be first. Everyone, assemble at the firing range."

When the men were standing side by side with

their weapons, Nat Baha walked down the line inspecting each man's rifle. He found them all clean and in good order. He required and expected this, but these were not combat blooded soldiers who had learned from experience. Mistakes would be made. Still, these AK 47s had all just undergone a thorough work over by Mr. Suliman. They should be in excellent condition.

He was also checking each man's general weapons discipline. Safeties were engaged, no fingers on triggers, each man ready, with his weapon secured from accidental discharge. He took Jahander's assault rifle and walked out in front of the men.

"Brothers, you have been practicing with semi-automatic feed. This provides you with a possible rate of fire of up to forty rounds per minute. Your rifle has a single magazine holding thirty rounds of 7.62 x 39 cartridges. With the two magazines taped together as yours are, you have sixty rounds available. You have been taught when the first magazine is empty, disengage it and flip it over to introduce the replacement magazine, like this." He quickly demonstrated, throwing the bolt and charging the weapon. "Can you do that on the run, Mr. Khalid?"

"Yes sir, I can. We all can."

"Good. You must become more proficient at it. It will not be possible for you to carry more than a few extra magazines hidden under your clothing or in a backpack. Movement is essential. You must begin firing even as you are moving. Don't stop. You have all practiced doing this. I cannot over-emphasize the importance of movement. The faster you are moving the better. It will be difficult for anyone to interfere with you or shoot back at you, if you are moving. Also, as you move through the crowd, more targets become exposed. Observe!"

Nat Baha spun to his left and trotted past the berm where a line of targets were set up. It was evident he had selected fully automatic feed for the weapon. It chattered as he ran, spent brass shells flying. He only ran the thirty or so yards down the line, but he never stopped firing. At the end of the line, he whirled as he traded magazines and trotted back up the line, firing again.

He stopped in front of the men ejecting the second spent magazine.

"Your weapons now have the capability to fire about one hundred rounds per minute. Who can tell me what the problem is?" he asked.

Aaron Parviz spoke up.

"You ran through all sixty rounds in less than fifty seconds. Your gun's empty and you're out of ammo. I doubt you were able to hit much of anything."

Baha's smile was without mirth.

"Exactly so, my brother. It takes great skill and control to be able to run like that and fire the weapon with any accuracy. Without expertise, a fully automatic weapon is only useful for spraying crowds and making people take cover. You might kill a few people by accident, but it is not as effective as selecting targets and taking them out with short, controlled bursts. Short bursts are better. Select a target and fire three to six rounds, then select another target."

He handed the hot weapon back to Jahander Khalid, along with two magazines he produced from under his shirt.

"You see, I was not without ammunition after all. Take your positions on the firing line."

When the men stepped into their individual shooting stations, they stopped and stared down range for a moment.

Aaron Parviz let out a long whistle between his teeth.

"Man, I take it back. That's some damned good shooting."

At his machine shop, Abdul Suliman had cut the six silhouette targets from half-inch thick steel plate, in roughly the shape of a standing man. The targets were currently set at twenty-five yards from the firing line. Each of the freshly painted targets now showed multiple bullet strikes. No target had less than five hits, all of them in the torso section of the target.

"I make that about thirty hits. Half your shots hit home. You would've probably killed all six." Aaron said.

"Yes. Unfortunately, Brother Parviz is correct. As he said, I wasted half of my ammunition and only killed six. Learn from this. Short bursts truly are better."

When he was satisfied the men had improved both in technical shooting application and strategic target acquisition, he dismissed them to clean their assault rifles. He instructed them to meet in the barn in thirty minutes.

When they were once again assembled, he told them the news.

"My brothers, there has been a change in plans. Our target must be shifted. We have been asked if the band would be interested in going on tour with this musician, Kyle Coltrane, and his band. There are certain strategic benefits to this opportunity. Imagine being able to travel the country without alerting the security services. Imagine being able to choose targets near each city in which the band performs. After a concert we could strike a target and be back on the tour bus within minutes. Within an hour after an attack, we could be miles away, taking our leisure on the bus, while chaos ensues behind us. It could take weeks for the authorities to make a connection. As you all know, we were going to use the up-coming concert as the launch point of our operations. Because of this new opportunity, I am planning a strike elsewhere. Your training is incomplete. None of you have seen any action yet. None of you are blooded. A smaller target with less security and better escape options may be more appropriate for the first strike. I'm finalizing the logistics and arranging for transportation. Prepare yourselves. Inch' Allah, we will strike the neck of America within days."

CHAPTER 29

Tony came by the office and, after spending some time with Christine, sat down in front of my desk.

"I thought you might like an update on the Ferguson case."

"Sure, what's up?"

"Bob Ferguson confessed. By the time we got him into interrogation he was ready to tell us everything."

"It's funny isn't it? You were right about him, Tony. You said you didn't think he would answer any questions if you confronted him, or tried to interview him in an official capacity. You asked me to talk to him at home because he'd feel more secure and empowered in his own environment. In his mind, I was just an employee. I wasn't sure he would crack. But he did."

"It was up to you to talk his wife into going along with it. It wasn't easy for her to make that choice. I've seen dozens of cases like this where the wife won't cooperate with us."

"Often, they can't, Tony. They want to, but they're too afraid. Fear is crippling. She had been living with shame and fear for so long, it's a wonder she was able to overcome it, even just one time. I think her anger fueled her strength, but anger can also do tremendous harm. It can become hate and bitterness. She'll need help to get past that."

"Too bad she didn't get angry sooner. Her daughter would be alive, and they all would've gotten the help they needed. At least now the sick freak will go to prison for the rest of his life."

"We're all sick, Tony. That's why we call Jesus "The great physician". He helps us diagnose our condition and, by his stripes, we are healed."

"When I think about Bob Ferguson, my blood boils. Don't you sometimes think, hell isn't hot enough?"

"Sure, but my concern is avoiding the place myself, and then helping other people do the same. I don't get to judge others, Tony. That's up to God."

"Right, I know. Still when I think about what he did..."

"Better to move on. Can you imagine what it must've been like for Priscilla Davidson? Rosie told her she's been sexually abused by her father for about ten years. Poor Priscilla was keeping that secret. She also knew Jimmy never hit or hurt Rosie in any way. When Bob Ferguson found out Rosie was dating Jimmy, he went ballistic. He was the one who put his own daughter in the hospital.

Think what it must've been like for Mrs. Ferguson to live with that guy. People cope with horrible things in their lives, often suffering in silence. I'm reminded to be sensitive to people's hurts. That's what I want to dwell on, being more compassionate. I tend to forget people are hurting, and sometimes when they act out it's an expression of their pain."

"I hear that. I guess being a cop has made me a little rough around the edges."

"You're like a tree, Tony. Your bark is thick and rough, but on the inside..."

"Yeah, but on the inside – I'm solid as an oak."

"OK, let's go with that. Speaking of going, I have an appointment I have to get to."

"Yes, you do, a lunch date with a certain dark-haired beauty."

"Now where did you hear...? Christine told you!"

CHAPTER 30

Walking into the restaurant, all eyes were on us. I knew it was the woman next to me who drew the attention.

Hafsah was now dressed in blue jeans and a grey tee-shirt, with the slogan "just do it" on the front. She was wearing blue, high-top sneakers. Her glistening dark hair was pulled back in a loose pony tail. As usual, her makeup was tasteful and flawless.

As soon as we were seated, she reached across the table and took hold of my hands.

"John, I'm sorry. Christine told me about the death of your friend last week. Now I understand why you are so adamant about not being a federal agent. I had no idea you were recently involved in anything so complex and difficult. I can't imagine how you are able to help with my mission and still handle your other cases, all while dealing with the grief and loss caused by the rogue FBI unit."

"Our mission, Hafsah, it's our mission to stop your cousin. I'm, sorry I haven't been able to focus exclusively on it. There are many changes happening, and I've been distracted and introspective. I can see more clearly now and I'm ready to take him down."

"We have to find him first. The trap is set for Monday, John. There is nothing we can really do today or on the weekend. We have already booked the studio space for next week. Christine is arranging for some promotional radio advertising, announcing the auditions. They will be broadcast all weekend. I will pick up the flyers and posters from the print shop this afternoon. My team and I will distribute them tomorrow. You need to rest and reflect. I believe this matter with the FBI is not yet concluded."

"You referred to Special Agent Booker as a 'rogue agent'. I'm not sure it's an accurate description. Although he was the Special Agent in Charge, he's answerable to someone above him. He may be just the tip of the iceberg. I suspect there is something bigger, uglier, and more sinister beneath the surface. Tony says we have enough evidence against Doug and his team to get them all indicted on multiple charges of murder and conspiracy to commit murder. Doug didn't seem even a little worried about it, and we don't actually know who all was on that team."

Hafsah picked up a menu.

"I doubt you will ever know. It would not be the first time your government found a way to cover up something ugly. If you cannot identify the agents who did the shooting, you cannot charge them with the crime."

I shrugged, picking up my menu.

"Someone knows who they are. We know for sure who one of the shooters was, SAIC Doug Booker. Everybody knows who he is and that he was in charge of the whole operation. Doug has his tail in the wringer. He's probably in D.C. answering some hard questions, as we speak."

Hafsah looked at me over the top of her menu.

"… Tale in the ringer? What does this mean?" She asked.

I couldn't help it. The question had caught me off guard, and struck me as funny. I started laughing.

Hafsah put down the menu, embarrassed.

"I'm sorry, Hafsah. It was a strange thing for me to say. I'm afraid the reference is rather obscure. Before people had electric or gas driers for their laundry, they would take the wet clothes out of the rinse water and run them through a wringer (I made a cranking motion with my hand) to squeeze out the excess water..."

Hafsah's face brightened. "Of course, if you were an animal like a cat or dog, having your tail in a wringer would be very painful."

"Yes, and you wouldn't be able to get away from it."

"Yes, I see that. Now, what were we talking about?" She batted her eyelashes at me, and I no longer cared what we had been talking about.

"You need a break, John. I'm looking forward to the concert tomorrow night, even if it is not a real date." She said, playfully.

"Hafsah, could you have someone on your team go pick up those fliers and posters? I'd like to spend the rest of the day with you. Would you call that a real date?"

Hafsah smiled. "Yes, John, a real date. I will enjoy that, very much." She gestured, indicating the restaurant. "This is, in point of fact, the start of our second date. You may recall, I had to invite you to the picnic."

I remembered the picnic, and the slap. I guess I wasn't the first man to have a date end with a slap. Perhaps things would go better this time.

After lunch, we went to the Caldwell Zoo. We walked hand in hand along the trails from one exhibit to the next, basking in the warm fall afternoon. Sitting on a bench, we watched the otters glide effortlessly through the water. We fed the ducks, and wandered around without any agenda. At the exhibit of animals on the African savannah, we observed the jackals. I couldn't help thinking of

Nat Baha. We were hunting him, even as he was stalking his prey. This moment was stolen from the hunt. While we were wandering around enjoying each other's company, Baha was drawing ever closer to his objective. The clock was ticking. Time was running out. If we didn't find him within the next few hours or days, he would kill again.

We purchased snow cones from the concession stand. Hafsah told me she had never seen or heard of snow cones. I found that hard to believe. I've had snow cones or shaved ice on three different continents, even in Southeast Asia.

I didn't want the afternoon to end. I didn't want to think about what had to be done, but those thoughts were never far away. The weight of our responsibility was burdensome. I remembered that I had been instructed to cast all my burdens on Him. He alone knew the future. He alone could provide the guidance we so desperately needed. Inwardly I began to pray.

Still thanking God for sending Hafsah into my life, she caught me staring at her and blushed, grinning at me.

"A penny for your thoughts," She said.

"I was thinking my life is better with you in it."

"Oh my! That is worth much more than a single penny. I believe I owe you a kiss."

I collected that kiss, right there in front of the elephants, giraffes and warthogs.

After all, warthogs aren't easily offended.

As the shadows began to grow longer, I asked her if she would join me for dinner.

"Thank you, yes I will. I don't want to spend the evening without you. I don't want this day to end. What do you have in mind? I will have to change clothes if we're going in search of haute cuisine."

I thought that was a fantastic idea. We could

spruce up a bit and go somewhere nice for a romantic dinner. The whole concept was so far removed from my recent experience; I could barely remember what it would be like.

Shepherds are as human as anyone on earth, but we don't age the same way other people do. When we accept the call, we are changed. Not in any obvious way. No, it's a very subtle and cruel change. This change from ordinary person to Shepherd simply slows the aging process.

For other humans, a life span of three score years and ten is about average. A man might live about seventy years, more or less, from birth to death, barring any mortal injury or illness.

A Shepherd only ages about one year for every ten years other people live; perhaps only one month for every year of other's lives. We have more time to learn, more time to attain wisdom, and greater opportunity to fulfill our assignments to influence and preserve what is right and good. We maintain the course of human events as has been ordained by our King.

Our original genetic predisposition, the effects of the environment, diet, nutrition and lifestyle have much less impact on our bodies. When injured, our bodies heal both more quickly and more fully.

If we accept the calling, we sacrifice the normal life as experienced by more ordinary people. With the exception of disease, we can be killed in any and all of the ways other people are, but our natural life span can be more than ten times that of the people around us.

This is the wonder and the horror of the change. Because of our slowed aging, we have to watch everyone around us deteriorate and die. After going through the grieving process early in the Twentieth Century, I had avoided becoming too close to a woman… until now.

People who meet me tend to think I'm in my thirties. I was called to become a Shepherd on the day of my twenty first birthday –– one hundred and fifty five years ago. I saw the birth of commercial flight, radio, television, computers, ubiquitous telephones - all of them, supermarkets, even fast food. Everyone I ever knew, prior to the time of my calling, has been dead for nearly a century.

It's been a while since I courted a gal.

After we left the zoo I dropped Hafsah at her hotel to dress for dinner, then I drove to my apartment to do the same. As I opened the door my phone rang. I recognized the number.

"Hey, Jack. What's up?"

"Can you meet in an hour?"

"No. I just walked into my apartment. I have another commitment. If you want to talk, come here."

He was silent for a second. I was about to ask if he was still there, when he spoke up.

"OK. I'll be there in ten minutes."

He hung up.

CHAPTER 31

Exactly ten minutes after Jack's phone call, he was standing in my front room. He wasn't there to admire my collection of old paintings and sculpture, or lounge about on the antique furniture. As usual, he got straight to the point.

"I think we may be onto something." He said.

I had to smile.

"Well, if DHS isn't onto something, we're all in a world of hurt."

"Right, 'Chuckles'. The point is, we may have a lead on where Muktallah is."

"Where?"

"There's a hunting camp out in the deep woods. We've tracked a couple of these subjects out of town by monitoring the GPS in a guy's truck. We have satellite imagery of the camp. Can't tell who is who, but there's a shooting range, and our subjects go there to shoot. At first, we figured it was just something guys do. Rifle season is right around the corner. Then we thought, what if? It looks like a training camp. The thing is, we can't follow anyone directly there without the risk of being made. If we spook these guys, it might delay their plans, but it won't stop them."

"You could just raid the camp. They may have computers, weapons and who knows what out there.

If Muktallah's there, you'll get him. I'd think you'd want to hit that place for sure."

"None of these dudes have committed a crime. Going out to a hunting camp, and doing some target practice just before deer season is perfectly legal. If we raid the camp and don't turn up anything, we've blown our chance to catch these guys."

"So, have a team sneak in there. Have a little look around. Maybe you'll flush the big bird."

"We need to send someone in there. I thought maybe you and your friend from overseas, might want to take a run at it. You could pretend you're a couple who got lost while bird watching or something."

I shook my head.

"Send in a game warden. It wouldn't be at all weird for a game warden to show up at a hunting camp. Be the perfect cover to have a look around. They're federal, so they can go anywhere at any time."

"Of course! Why didn't I think of that?"

"Typically, you professional spooks tend to think along espionage and counter terrorism lines. The straight up, in your face approach isn't in the spymaster playbook."

"See, that's why we need you. You're just a plain old country boy at heart."

"You don't need me, Jack. You're just using me. There's a difference."

"My, aren't we touchy? What's the problem stud, not getting any?"

I didn't mean to, but I hit him pretty hard.

Jack hadn't been expecting it, so it was kind of a cheap shot. It shook him, but he didn't go down. He spun toward me, ducked and launched a kick at my head. I blocked it with my left forearm and stepped back away from him before he could follow through with another attack.

"Stop it! I'm sorry, Jack. I shouldn't have hit you. It was uncalled for."

He was in a combat stance, ready for the fight. He straightened up and rolled his head around, twisting his neck.

"Damn, John. You used to hit better than that."

"I mean it, Jack. I shouldn't have done that. I'm sorry. Let me get you some ice."

There was already some swelling starting on his cheek just in front of his left ear.

He put his fingers to the side of his face.

"Yeah, some ice would be good." He said.

I found a bag of frozen peas in the freezer and tossed it to him.

"Seriously, you used to hit harder. Did you pull that punch?" he asked, placing the bag of peas on the side of his face.

I nodded.

"Too little, too late, I don't even know why I hit you."

"Ahh, don't worry about it. You've got more than enough reasons. I should learn better manners. I tend to speak without thinking. We cool?"

I shrugged.

"We're cool. Again, I'm sorry, Jack."

"You won't mind if I take this with me?" He held up the bag of frozen peas.

I grinned at him.

"Consider it a donation to the cause. Let me know what you learn from the game warden."

"Don't worry, pal. I'll keep you in the loop. You do the same for me."

When he was gone, I thought about our meeting. Once again, he was playing me. I resented it. His improper comment had irritated me. It was no excuse, but there it was.

When he 'had run his mouth, I had lost control. I hadn't done that since the last time he 'had pushed me too far, about a decade ago.

I wasn't sure what he was up to, but whatever it was, it stank of political manipulation. That was his problem. My problem was my attitude. I needed to confess my sin. Jack was the one who had been hit, but I was the one who had to repent. I wondered which was the more painful.

I took Hafsah to dinner at a restaurant about twelve miles south of Tyler. The South African owner called it Kiepersol. The story was something about some men on a safari who were treed by a Cape buffalo. "How long will we have to stay up in this tree?" One of them asked the native guide. "It is hard to say. All night, a couple of days, who knows? Even if he goes away, he may wait nearby. When we come down, he might charge and plow us into a bloody rut." The guide said.

"Oh Lord, keep us all." One of the men said. That's the story. At least that's sort of the way the story goes. No matter how the name came about, the atmosphere and cuisine was as good as could be hoped for, anywhere in Texas

So was my dinner date.

"Oh my, John, that is quite a stretch." Hafsah said, after listening to the story.

Changing the subject, I asked, "Will you be dressed in traditional attire for the concert tomorrow night?"

"Yes, John. That was the original plan, and I still think it best to maintain the charade. Aaron Parviz expects to see me there. If we really are permitted to go behind the stage, I must keep up appearances."

"Sure, but if something goes wrong, you won't be ready for a fight."

Hafsah rolled her eyes.

"John, if there is to be a fight, I promise you how I am dressed will not determine the outcome. I can fight naked if it comes down to it."

I'm blessed with a rich imagination.

It was my turn to blush.

CHAPTER 32

It was another typically hot East Texas afternoon. Baha and Suliman were in the cargo container organizing equipment to put into a rental truck they would use to transport the band's gear to the concert. There was a storage building on the outskirts of Tyler, housing most of the bulky sound equipment and set decoration the Honky Tonk Broncs used on stage. This cargo container stored the weapons and more specialized equipment they used in training, and for the upcoming operation. They still planned to take weapons to the concert.

It was nearly stifling in the storage container. Nat Baha used the sleeve of his shirt to wipe sweat away from his face as he closed a guitar case. His thoughts drifted back to how he had come to be in this horribly humid place.

He had always had a penchant for violence. Like a common house cat, he was a natural born killer. Unlike a domestic tabby, he was born in the right time and place to develop his skills and feed his need. He knew he was special — different from most other people. While he didn't understand the relationship between cutting down countless strangers and finding his muse, he felt it within himself. He drew upon a hidden well of pathos mixed with malice, pouring it out in the sound emanating from his guitars.

Having taken so many souls, enriched by the anguish he had caused, he distilled it into notes plucked from guitar strings. Although he never spoke of it, he thought of his music as the sound of stolen lives.

When he was younger, he had feared he might be insane. Surely his peculiar lusts and needs could not be normal, could they? Over time, his angel had shown him he was not insane, but set apart for a special purpose. He was extraordinarily gifted, both musically and in his forbidden vocation as a killer.

He was a chosen servant of Allah.

Nat Baha was also given special dreams. Sometimes the angel appeared in his dreams and told him strange and wonderful things, dark things. At first, he would awaken from his dream with only wisps and wafts of memory, the images and events driven away by the light of day. With the passing years the dreams had become more vivid. Lately they had become more frequent. In his dreams he received direction. Because he believed he was doing a holy work, he also believed Allah had sent his messenger to guide him. He believed the angel was Gabriel. Was this not the same angel who had appeared to the Prophet? Had he not been directed to this place by the angel?

Perhaps here, his dreams of fame and fortune might well align with the more ominous dreams the angel inspired. He had begun to feel the presence of the angel, even in daylight. Sometimes he thought he saw Gabriel out of the corner of his eye, but could never be sure.

Thinking these things, Nat Baha was certain the concert would go as planned. Everything would go as planned.

Suliman spoke up, interrupting his thoughts.

"A woman came to see me at the shop. She said she was an interior designer. She showed me photographs of copper and bronze vessels she wanted to have converted into lamps. You know pitchers, vases and the like. Some of them were pretty cool looking."

Baha scowled at him.

"Is there a point to this story?"

"It just struck me as odd. She wanted to see where the work would be done and what type of equipment I used."

Again, wiping away sweat, Baha shrugged.

"The thing is, she reminded me of the description Aaron gave us of the woman he met at the convenience store. She's beautiful with dark eyes and complexion, a brilliant smile…"

"Is that so uncommon?"

"It is in my machine shop. There's something else, too. She had an accent. She wasn't born American. I'd bet my life on it."

Before Nat Baha could comment, they heard a call from somewhere outside. "Hello! Is anyone here?"

Nat Baha produced his Glock without thinking of it. Just before switching off the light, he motioned for Suliman to go out and intercept whoever was out there.

He eased farther back into the darkness as Suliman stepped out into the yard. Baha heard him address the intruder.

"Hello. What can I do for you?"

"Good afternoon. I'm Tom Vincent, the Game Warden. I just need to have a look around. Bow hunting season starts tomorrow. Y'all haven't been hunting, have you?"

"Nope. We aren't even bow hunters. We're just getting the camp squared away for rifle season."

"Is there someone else here with you?"

"No, just me."

"You said 'we'. Who's here with you?"

"What I mean is, there are several of us on the lease. I'm here alone today, but we've all pitched in to get things ready."

"Uh huh. Can I see some ID, maybe your hunting license?"

"Sure, but it's in the house there. Can I offer you a cup of coffee?"

"… Sounds good. I just need to look in the container first."

"Uh, why's that?"

"… Just doing my job. OK?"

"I guess."

As the game warden stepped out of the brightly lit yard, it took a moment for his eyes to adjust to the darkness within the container. Nat Baha had the man's silhouette in the front site of the Glock.

When the game warden realized what he was seeing, his hand dropped for his service weapon, but it was too late.

Nat Baha shot him three times. The roar of the gunfire inside the container was deafening. The game warden pitched over backwards with his arms flung out to the sides. He landed on his back in the yard, gasping for breath, his eyes staring up at the few puffy clouds in the fall sky. Nat Baha walked out of the container and shot him in the face.

He looked over at Suliman and said, "This place is burned. We must clear out all our things and move to the secondary location."

"I'll say! Man, you just killed a fed. They'll be looking for us under every rock and tree leaf."

Scanning the area, Nat Baha nodded.

"There is no time to properly dispose of the body. We'll leave him to the buzzards. Bring the truck around, we must get moving."

CHAPTER 33

The Kyle Coltrane concert was sold out. Somehow, Christine had arranged for the four of us to have tickets and VIP passes. Like eels slipping through gaps in a net, we slid through the milling mass of closely packed humanity to where we were to be seated. Our seats were just off the center aisle, three rows back from the edge of the stage. For me, the recorded music was already too loud. We were too close to the huge banks of speakers flanking the stage. Nobody else seemed to mind.

It was clear any conversation would have to be limited to a few shouted words, or acted out in pantomime.

Hafsah had been true to her word. She wore a nearly floor length, long sleeved dress of embroidered silk, in a color I would call 'peach'. She also wore the same opaque white hijab I had seen before. Tonight, it was pulled up over her head and pinned beneath her chin. Somehow, the hijab framing her face made her look even more beautiful. I had been sensitive to the stares we got as we worked our way through the crowd. Most people were just curious, a few were admiring, but some were openly hostile.

I reminded myself there are pinheads everywhere.

We found our assigned seats. We had four together, on the end of a row. Tony indicated Hafsah and I should take the inside seats. I was in the fourth seat, with Hafsah on my right. Christine was seated next to Hafsah, with Tony next to her in the aisle seat. Christine was dressed in jeans and boots, with a blue 'Guns N Roses' T-Shirt tucked into the jeans, her radiant red hair, loose about her shoulders. The cultural distance between the appearances of the two remarkable women seated next to each other was staggering. I had to smile. You might say the four of us represented guns and roses. I knew the gun under Tony's jacket had nothing to do with roses and nobody wanted to hear it sing. They didn't want to hear the sound of mine either. There was no question the ladies were as beautiful and different from each other as any roses ever seen.

Presently, a guy and a gal walked out on stage. The crowd cheered and whistled.

The pair was well-loved local radio personalities, "Roarin' Randy & Rachel," they had the morning show on Hot Mix-106.

"Howdeeee!" Randy roared into the microphone, Rachel grinning beside him.

"Howdeeee!" The crowd roared back.

"Tonight we are going to party. Y'all know what to expect. KYLE COLTRANE is IN THE HOUSE!" Randy roared.

The crowd went wild.

Randy and Rachell clapped and grinned at each other for a moment, and then Randy continued his wind-up.

"But tonight, folks, tonight we're bringing you more than you expected. Tonight, we bring you the unexpected. Ladies and gents, put your hands together for…" He handed the microphone to Rachel, who announced, "Tyler's own house band, the Honky Tonk Broncs."

The curtains parted as Roarin' Randy & Rachel, left the stage. The crowd noise was so loud, for a moment we couldn't hear the rhythm being laid down by Aaron Parviz on the drums, with the three guitar players out front.

While the current trend with musicians was ultra-casual, baggy jeans and tee shirts being the norm, these guys had adopted more theatricality. There was some attention paid to costuming. The lead guitar player sported a big sombrero, like a mariachi or caballero might wear. His wide guitar strap had been converted into a bandolier with what appeared to be real 7.62 x 39 rifle cartridges in the bullet loops. With his dark complexion and his black beard and mustache, he looked the part of the bandito.

The rhythm guitar player wore a matador's cap and jacket, the jacket studded with crystals, sparkling colorfully in the spotlight.

The bass player had long hair and kept it pulled away from his face with a headband of a bright red kerchief tied behind his head. His green tank top and camouflage pants tucked into jungle boots completed the Rambo look.

Aaron Parvis had chosen to wear the plain white caftan and skull cap, the traditional garb for many men in the Muslim world.

They were good, surprisingly good. The opening number was kind of a throwback to the days of country/rock. They sounded a little bit like the Eagles with a touch of Lynyrd Skynyrd thrown in. I found myself tapping my foot involuntarily.

The rhythm guitar player was the lead singer, with the bass player backing him up. The vocals were tight. The bass player was steady and true, the rhythm guitar kept the sound alive, but the lead guitar player with the bandito get-up was something special. That guy wove a haunting stream of sound through the song, touching some primal part of the whole audience.

I was so captivated I wasn't paying much attention to those around me. I felt Hafsah grip my arm.

When I looked at her, her eyes were open wide. She was trying to tell me something.

I tried to read her lips. "That's him," she seemed to be saying, pointing at the lead guitarist.

It hit me like an on-coming train.

The bandito lead guitarist for the Honky Tonk Broncs, was none other than the international Islamic terrorist, Hakim Muktallah, now known as Nat Baha.

"Are you sure?" I mouthed at Hafsah.

She nodded her affirmative response, setting her mouth into a thin line.

Of course, she was sure. It just made sense. Tony told me about the suspected murder of the former lead guitarist. Now, here was Nat Baha, playing in his place. What a remarkable coincidence. Nat Baha wanted to get his music recorded, and suddenly there was an opening for a lead guitarist in a band that was clearly headed for the stars.

Hafsah and I stared at each other in shock.

Now what? We couldn't exactly rush the stage and grab him, or kill him in the middle of a rather excellent performance. How would that look?

We needed a plan, but we couldn't even discuss it under these circumstances.

I saw Christine looking at us with some curiosity.

I turned my attention back to the stage as the band ended the first song to a thunderous round of applause and whistles. The momentary quiet as the crowd noise died down gave me just a second to speak to Hafsah.

"Let's go get some air." I suggested, as the band started the next tune.

Hafsah nodded and turned to speak to Christine, who turned to speak to Tony. Tony looked annoyed, but he stood up to let us out, as did Christine.

It suddenly dawned on me, if we walked out at this moment, every eye in the venue would be on us. Hafsah would be particularly noticed. I grabbed her arm just as she started to stand and shook my head at Tony. Tony gave me a quizzical look, but changed it to resignation and he and Christine sat down again.

This musical offering was a ballad, a tender love song, accompanied by a light lead guitar that gently picked at our heartstrings and left notes hanging in the air. It was much quieter than the first song, which gave me opportunity to speak directly into Hafsah's ear.

"We can't be seen walking out on this performance," I looked at her eyes to see if she understood.

She closed them and nodded her understanding. When she opened her eyes, there was a fire blazing there. I had seen this before, right before we broke into the machine shop, and a little earlier, when she slapped me.

She leaned in to speak into my ear. I was half expecting another slap.

"We'll kill him during the intermission." She said.

"We'll see…" I mouthed back at her.

Hafsah set her mouth in a thin line. I could see she was working on a plan, a plan that might or might not include me. She had promised to take her cousin alive, if it could be done. Her body language and facial expression suggested she now intended a different outcome. She pulled her cell phone out of her purse and began typing furiously. I figured she was sending a text to her team.

CHAPTER 34

To say the musical set the Honky Tonk Broncs played was well received, would be a serious understatement. Their performance and song choices were superb. The incorporation of the new lead guitar player was, well – instrumental.

He played three or four different guitars over the course of the set. In the third song and later, in the final song, Nat Baha played lead guitar solos that were stunning. At times he was ripping riveting riffs, shredding it. At other times his playing took us on voyages of imagination.

I was amazed. This guy was gifted and he had practiced his craft, refining and fine tuning it to the point of genius. No wonder he wanted to get his music recorded. What a waste of God's gift. He might've used his gift to bring honor and glory to his Creator; instead he had turned the passion and fire God had given him into a tool of the devil.

His music was celestial; his life's work was diabolical.

I had noticed Tony slipping out during the final song.

With a crescendo at the end of their closing number The Honky Tonk Broncs brought down the house. The crowd went nuts, as the curtain closed.

Roarin' Randy & Rachel came out on the stage,

waving the crowd to quiet down.

"Howdeee," Randy roared.

"Howdeee," the crowd roared back.

"Wow, I mean… WOW! Am I right?" Roarin' Randy asked.

There was a thunderous applause, punctuated by whistles, in response.

"Yep, I hear you, and I think the whole world is gonna be hearing some of that!"

I could feel the tension and energy building in Hafsah to the point of her being ready to leap up out of her seat.

The crowd agreed with Roarin' Randy. As they settled down, he told us he and Rachel had a special announcement.

"Ladies and gents, we've been asked by a member of the Tyler Police department, if he could have just a moment to ask a question. Let's welcome him onto the stage. Ladies and gents, I give you… Lieutenant Tony Escalante."

Randy & Rachel pumped up the crowd as Tony walked out to the microphone.

Christine, Hafsah, and I all looked at each other, wondering what in the world Tony was doing on the stage.

He looked terrified, but his voice didn't waiver. He was blinded by the spotlight, but he looked over in our general direction.

"Hey folks, thank you for giving me this moment. I have only one question, the most important question I've ever asked in my life… Christine Valakova; will you marry me?"

The spot light lit up Christine, Hafsah and me, in the process.

For just a moment, Christine was so stunned and shocked, she was frozen. The crowd was silent with anticipation.

Suddenly, she grinned and yelled.

"… Of course, I will, you big gorilla!"

And… the crowd went wild.

One of the security people led Christine to the stairs, from which she rushed onto the stage and into Tony's arms, where they kissed in front of several thousand of their closest friends.

Hoopla ensued.

This was the perfect moment for Hafsah and me to leave our seats. We went to the security guy and showed him our VIP passes. He took us through a side door putting us in a corridor where several people were traveling to and from some restrooms.

Through the walls, we could hear the muffled sound of Roarin' Randy doing his wind-up to introduce the headliner, Kyle Coltrane.

I asked someone where we might find the guys from Honky Tonk Broncs.

"Get in line, seems like everybody wants to meet those guys. Go over there to that second door. It'll take you backstage. Somebody back there will point you in the right direction."

I pulled Hafsah aside.

"This is not the time or the place." I told her.

Hafsah made a face, her frustration clearly evident. She bobbed her head once, in acknowledgement.

"I mean it, Hafsah. There are too many people here. Too many witnesses and too many who could get hurt. Tell me you understand."

She met my eyes.

"Yes, John. This is not the time or the place. We are so close, but we must proceed with caution. I understand. You can trust me."

I squeezed her shoulder.

"OK, then. Let's go find Nat Baha."

We went down the corridor and through the second door. The sound and activity were nearly overwhelming. There were roadies, technicians, stage hands, set dressers, and people whose functions were unclear, rushing around behind the stage. One man was moving the drum set that belonged to the Honky Tonk Broncs. Out on the stage, we caught a brief glimpse of Kyle Coltrane's profile, lit by the spot lights. Behind him and his band, there were fog machines and fans, laser lights whipping around, and a huge screen with images of flames and horses running across it. The crowd was rocking the place. Coltrane's band began to play. The noise level was intense.

We made our way through and around the workers and found Tony and Christine entwined directly behind the giant screen, the light of the flames illuminating them in shades of yellow, orange and red. I was reminded for a moment of the images from the night a farm house had burned while I watched helplessly. Tony put his hands over his ears and then pointed at a door in the opposite wall. We all hustled in that direction, not much concerned about where it might lead. Anywhere quieter had to be better.

We went through the door and found ourselves in another corridor. Although we could still hear Kyle Coltrane and company, performing less than twenty-five yards behind us, it was much quieter here.

This corridor was filled with people who appeared to have an interest in Kyle Coltrane or his band members. Some were probably family and friends. Others were members of the media or in the music business. The rest were probably groupies or folks like us, just wanting to meet the musicians.

I turned to Tony and shook his hand.

"Congratulations, Tony. You got the girl. That was some proposal, by the way. It took guts. I could tell, because you looked a little green around the gills. I believe you achieved your goal in spectacular style. She'll never forget this night."

"Thanks, J.W." He said, grinning from ear to ear.

Hafsah and I kissed Christine on the cheek. We

wished her well and invoked God's blessing on both of them and their marriage.

"How about we all go somewhere and celebrate." Tony suggested, beaming.

"Don't you want to go back and see the Kyle Coltrane concert?" I asked.

"Naw, not really. What could be better than this?" Christine was in full agreement.

"It sounds like a great idea, Tony. How about Hafsah and I meet you somewhere? We have some business to attend to."

"Business? Tonight? Come on, J.W., get with the program." Tony said.

"We will. You and Christine go on. We'll meet you as soon as we can."

Tony and Christine studied us for a moment.

"J.W., is this serious? Do you need some back-up?" Tony asked.

"No, Tony. This is part of something we've been working on for a while. We just need to meet somebody, briefly. We'll be along right after that."

Tony said, "OK, then. We'll go get a table somewhere and give you a call. Don't be long. We might not wait on you."

I could tell he was concerned.

"Super. I'm looking forward to it." I said.

"Yes, I am as well." Hafsah added.

I shook Tony's hand again, and they turned toward an exit sign farther down the corridor.

Christine turned back.

"Is this part of that thing I don't need to know about?" She asked.

"You don't need to know, Christine." I said.

She tilted her head for a moment, about to say something, but then she turned back toward the exit, in step with Tony.

I turned to Hafsah.

"Well then, I guess it's time for us to meet your cousin."

"It is past time." She replied.

CHAPTER 35

We asked where we might find the Honky Tonk Broncs, and were directed down the corridor to an unmarked door where several people were milling about, apparently waiting to get in.

There was a security guy standing outside the door, so we headed straight to him.

"Hello, this is Nadia Ahmed, and I'm Earl Hightower, with Harmotech Records. Aaron Parviz is expecting us."

The security guy was intrigued by Hafsah.

"What did you say your name was?" He asked her.

"Nadia Ahmed.".

"Nadia Ahmed." He repeated. He pointed at me. "Hightower, right?"

I nodded my affirmative.

"Please tell Mr. Parviz I am here." Nadia said.

"Nadia Ahmed." The security guy repeated.

Hafsah gave him a dazzling smile. "Yes. That is very good. Thank you"

The security guy nodded and went through the door, closing it behind him.

I knew the people who worked security at these venues were usually bouncers in clubs or off duty cops. This guy was a bouncer.

He was only gone about a minute. When he came back out, he held the door open for "Nadia". I started to follow her in, but he held up his hand.

"Just the lady, pal." He said.

Hafsah smiled at him again. "It is alright. He is with me."

The security guy shrugged and I stepped past him, following Hafsah inside. The security guy had just let an armed man through the door, all because of a fake name and a pretty woman's smile.

Inside we were immediately greeted by Aaron Parviz, who rose off a couch where he had been seated next to Nat Baha, sans the sombrero and bandolier guitar strap. A quick scan of the room told me there were about a dozen people inside. There were the four musicians, six visitors of one kind or another and the two of us.

The room itself was unremarkable. It was appointed as a dressing room/living space, but could be quickly converted to another purpose. In the living space, the furniture consisted of a couch, two upholstered chairs and a coffee table. At the far end of the room was a huge lighted mirror above a long counter with folding chairs in front of it. The counter top held the usual assortment of cosmetics and associated sponges and tissues, etc. that were ubiquitous in dressing rooms. Against one wall there was a metal locker and a free-standing clothes rack with a shelf on top. Most of the costume accoutrements were all hanging there, the sombrero and the matador hat on the shelf. There was a door in another wall I figured probably led to a restroom.

All the other people in the room were standing and conversing. They checked us out with a glance as we came in.

Aaron Parviz was still dressed in the traditional garb he had worn on stage.

"Hello, Nadia. I'm so glad to see you." Parviz said, putting an arm around her waist and turning her toward the couch.

Hafsah stiffened at his intimate touch. I could see Nat Baha was offended by this inappropriate violation of the teaching of the Prophet. In Islam there are strict rules about how men and women are to interact in public, especially as it relates to touching. He was displeased with his associate.

He glanced at me.

Nadia began making introductions.

"Aaron, this is my friend Earl Hightower. He is a record producer. He is very impressed with the band." Hafsah said, as she stepped away from Parviz' unwelcome closeness.

"How do you do?" Parviz mumbled. He ignored my offered handshake. "Nadia, I want you to meet Nat Baha, our lead axe. Nat, this is my friend Nadia Ahmed."

"As-salamu alayka, sister." Nat Baha said, inclining his head toward Hafsah. He didn't bother to get up from the couch.

"Wa alaikum assalam wa rahmatu Allah." Hafsah replied.

Nat Baha seemed pleased by this response. He looked over at me.

"As-salamu alayka." He said, with the same nod of his head.

"Uhh, thank you, Mr. Baha." I replied.

"A pity you don't speak Arabic, Mr. Hightower. How do you do?" Baha said, with a patient smile.

"I'm real pleased to meet you. That was a stellar performance, simply stellar." I said, reaching across the coffee table to shake his hand. I intended to be the personification of obsequiousness.

"Aaron, you have been rude to our guests. Shake Mr. Hightower's hand. Is this not the teaching of the Prophet? Salla Allaahu 'alayhi wa salaam." Baha instructed.

"Of course, please excuse me, Mr. Hightower. This is a big night for us, and I suppose I've forgotten my manners." Parviz said, offering his hand.

We shook.

"Please be seated." Baha said, indicating the two unoccupied chairs.

Hafsah and I sat down. I observed she had her hands folded in her lap and her eyes were slightly downcast whenever she looked in Nat Baha's direction.

"Perhaps our guests would like some tea. Mr. Hightower, I suppose you would prefer something stronger..." Nat Baha started.

"No, no. Thank you, no. We can't stay. We're on our way to meet some other folks for supper. Say, would y'all like to join us?" I offered.

I saw Hafsah cut her eyes at me.

"That would be delightful, I am sure, Mr. Hightower. Unfortunately, we cannot do so. We have been invited to join Mr. Coltrane on stage at the end of his performance. Perhaps another time..." Nat Baha answered.

"Yeah, about that, what do you say we get together and talk about getting this band a bigger audience?" I suggested.

"Again, we are otherwise occupied this evening." Baha reminded me.

"Sure, sure, I understand. I meant later on, sometime in the next couple of days."

"That is a possibility. May I have your card?"

I fumbled out my card case and handed him my generic business card. All that was on it was my usual fake name Mr. Earl Hightower, and a phone number. The card stock was excellent and the embossing was top shelf.

"Now, that number is my personal number. I always have that phone on me. You can reach me anywhere, anytime." I informed him.

"Next week, Mr. Hightower will be doing some business with the Superior Sound Systems studio, here in Tyler." Hafsah informed him.

Baha nodded.

"Listen, maybe I should be talking to your manager..." I said.

"Mr. Parviz is the founder of the band, and the business manager. Aren't you, Aaron?" Hafsah said, returning her attention to Aaron Parviz.

"Yeah, that's right."

"Well, fine then." I handed Parviz a card as well. "Boys, you give me a call. We can set this up."

The two men exchanged a look.

"Inch' Allah." Baha said.

"Is that a restaurant? Do you want to meet there?" I asked.

Baha smiled a tired smile.

"Americans, you never bother learning anything about other peoples, cultures, or languages. Perhaps we will meet again, if Allah wills it, Mr. Hightower."

"Good, that's good. Do you live here in Tyler, Mr. Baha?"

"I am a man of the world. Today I am here, to-morrow, who can say?" He replied.

I caught Hafsah's eyes as they flared a little.

"Well, I can promise you, if you can give us even a few days, we can make a demo you boys can be real proud of."

"Time will tell. Isn't that what you Americans say?" Baha said, standing up.

"Sure. Wait, are you saying you aren't an American?"

"I am a citizen of Islam, Mr. Hightower."

"Where's that?" I asked, feigning ignorance.

He stiffened and replied, "That is a discussion for another time.".

"OK, sure. It doesn't matter though. You don't have to be an American. You can play your guitar like nobody's business. That's what matters."

"Thank you for saying so. If you will forgive my rudeness, I must ask you to go. Indeed, Aaron, it is time to clear the room. We must prepare to go on stage."

No more than a minute later, we found ourselves out in the corridor with the other ousted visitors.

CHAPTER 36

Standing in the hallway outside the concert hall, I looked at my watch. I was analyzing the meeting we had just had with Nat Baha. I was sure he had been very interested in the opportunity to make a recording. It was clear to me there was little we could do by way of capturing him at this time, in this place.

Turning to Hafsah I tried to bring her around to my way of thinking.

"Well, we could go back to our seats, or head for the truck. We told Tony and Christine we would join them. Which would you prefer?"

Before she could answer, my phone buzzed. I saw Tony had texted me the name of the place we were supposed to meet them.

Hafsah had pulled her phone out and was typing a message.

"That was Tony. He told me where we should meet them. Let's head on over there." I suggested.

Hafsah looked at me with a strange, kind of distant look.

"Yes, you should do that."

"What did you say?"

"John, thank you so much for all you have done. I don't know if we would have been able to find him without your help. My team and I will take it from here. You should go meet your friends. Tell them I am very happy for them and give them my love."

"That's not going to happen…"

"Let's go outside, where we can talk more privately." She said. She turned and headed toward a big steel roll-up door at the far end of the corridor. Beside it, there was a smaller door under an exit sign. I hurried to catch up to her.

Outside, we found ourselves on a loading dock. There were two big cargo trucks and a smaller rental truck backed up to it. In the backs of the larger trucks we could see a couple of pieces of electrical equipment and piles of cables and moving blankets. The door of the smaller rental truck had been pulled closed. Clearly, this was the place where the band equipment was loaded and unloaded. The musicians would also come and go through here to avoid the crowds. Beyond the trucks were two, huge customized buses. Those would be the tour buses for Kyle Coltrane and his band. I figured the rental truck had to be what the Honky Tonk Bronc's were using. Out in the secure area where the tour buses were parked, there were a couple of dozen other vehicles.

Hafsah carefully studied all this.

"Yes, this is the place. We'll kill him here." She said, thinking out loud. She turned to me, not meeting my eyes.

"John, this is where I must leave you. My team and I will finish this. I must scout the area, Good bye." She turned away from me, headed for the stairs at the edge of the loading dock.

I grabbed her by the arm and spun her around to face me.

"No. Not like this. You don't get to just waive me off. We're in this together. We're meant to be together. Together in this, at least."

Hafsah met my eyes.

"No, John, I cannot ask you to do this," she choked.

"You promised me if there was a way, we would try to take him alive. Let's do that."

"I, I don't know..." she was searching my eyes.

"I do. Besides, there are only four of you, against four of them. If there is a fight, the odds are even. I'm your ace in the hole."

Hafsah looked confused.

Me and my idioms!

"There are only two men, John. My cousin Hakim, and Aaron Parviz." Hafsah observed.

That was why she looked confused.

"No, all four men are here, Hafsah. When we were backstage, I saw Abdul Suliman moving band equipment and Jahander Khalid was in the room talking to the other band members. Remember, you also promised to help stop all of them before they commit a terrorist act."

Hafsah nodded thoughtfully.

"This is going to be more complicated than I realized." She said.

"You need me and I need you."

She nodded and put her face against my shoulder. I wrapped her in my arms.

"See, we really do need each other." I whispered in her ear.

I was thinking about whether I should call Jack and alert him to what we had found. He probably had some DHS agents already on site. He had indicated he was planning to do so.

I concluded that after what happened at the farmhouse where my friend Gary was killed, I would never again trust the federal government or my old friend, Jack McCarthy.

Whatever was coming tonight, we would have to handle it without the aid of Uncle Sam.

Hafsah and I trotted down the stairs and out into the secure area where the tour buses were parked.

I figured the mix of cars, SUVs and pick-up trucks parked out there probably belonged to people working the show. Even this far away from the building, we could still hear the music, a steady rhythmic sound punctuated by wild crowd noise.

A set of headlights blinked on, then off.

Hafsah turned to me and said, "It is time for you to meet my team."

I didn't know how they had done it, but the black Chevy Tahoe which Hafsah and I had used when we went on the picnic, was now parked in the secure lot. Those were the headlights that flashed.

As we approached the vehicle, there was just enough light, I could see a figure in the driver's seat. Two people emerged from the shadows between the cars, one on each side of us.

I reached for my gun, but Hafsah put her hand on my arm.

"They are with me." She said. "David, Benjamin, this is John Wesley Tucker. John, this is David Goldstein and Benjamin Mordechai."

I shook hands with the men, who I now recognized from previous sightings.

"That's Anke Wolfe in the Tahoe." She said.

Hafsah indicated the driver should join us.

When the tall, blonde-haired woman approached us, Hafsah made the introduction. "John, this is Anke Wolfe. Anke, John Wesley Tucker."

"So, we finally meet the mystery man," Anke said, with a wink.

I didn't know for sure if she was referring to me or Muktallah/Baha.

"We have a little time. I'm going to change clothes. John, please tell them what you told me. Then, we must plan what we are to do." Hafsah headed to the back of the Tahoe and opened the hatch. I couldn't see what she was doing, but then I wasn't really supposed to be watching. I turned my attention to the three people near me.

"As you may know, Hakim Muktallah is inside the auditorium at this moment. Using the name Nat Baha, he's performing with the local band, the Honky Tonk Broncs." I checked my watch. "They will be on stage with the headliner, Kyle Coltrane, in about fifteen minutes. That will be the end of the concert. What you may not know is that Muktallah has trained with at least three local jihadists to commit acts of terrorism here in East Texas. You may have had eyes on a couple of those guys. All four of them are connected to the band, and are in the auditorium right now. There may also be others we don't know about.

Hafsah wanted to kill Muktallah as he came out of the auditorium, but once the concert is over there will be too many people coming out the back. We don't know if they will be armed. If you try to kill him and anything goes wrong, it could turn into a blood bath. Even if it is possible to single out Muktallah for assassination, it would leave the other members of his jihadist group to do whatever they have planned. We need a new plan."

"John is right." Hafsah said, emerging from behind the Tahoe. She now had her hair tied back, under a black baseball cap. She wore the dark grey t-shirt over the same grey urban camouflage cargo pants she had worn to the picnic.

"We can't risk an altercation here. There are four terrorists, not just one. We must hit them somewhere when there are fewer innocent bystanders."

"The others are not our concern, Hafsah. We came for Muktallah. We need to isolate him and take him out." David said.

"The mission has changed. We must take all of them. If we do not, the other jihadists will strike and kill countless numbers of innocent people. Muktallah has been our sole focus, because of what he has already done, yes, but we are also to prevent him from doing something similar to his past exploits, here in the United States. We were sent to stop him from killing Americans. Just killing Muktallah alone will not do anything to stop whatever they have planned to do. If we kill him and leave the rest, we will have failed in an important part of our mission."

"I've heard nothing of the sort from Jerusalem." David said.

"There has been no time to confirm this with Mossad. Muktallah is still our primary target, but we must stop the others as well. I have promised this to John."

Anke said, "I agree with Hafsah. She is the lead on this and, as always, the situation is fluid. We can't wait to hear what Jerusalem says. We must decide a course of action right now."

"Time is of the essence. We know where Muktallah is, at this moment. If it is too dangerous to try killing him as he emerges from the building, he is still our primary target. I say we follow him and take him out, tonight, as soon as possible. If we can get the others at the same time, it is good. If not, we alert the local authorities and let them handle it." Benjamin said.

Hafsah looked at me.

Whatever was to happen, it couldn't happen here. There were too many innocent lives endangered. If somehow the majority of the other people left the venue before the terrorists came out, we might get an opportunity. Otherwise, nearby, there were thousands of people who would be trying to leave the concert and get out on the roads.

"I think they'll wait until the crowds have gone, they'll load their equipment before they try to leave this place. Even so, there'll still be dozens of people coming out the back, and coming right where we are. Can you set up a sniper somewhere nearby to hit Muktallah, without endangering anyone else?"

We all scanned the area.

"No, if I could get on top of the building, I might get a shot, even from on top of one of those busses. But there is too little light, too little cover and, as you said, too many other people." David indicated.

"If he comes out here to a vehicle, can you converge on him as a group and take him down?" I asked.

Benjamin shook his head.

"That is unknown and difficult to prepare for. We don't know if he will be alone, what vehicle he might go to, or even if he will come out here."

"Well, we now have about ten minutes before the concert is over. Shortly after that, the back door of the building will slide open and people will be loading equipment and heading for their cars. We'd better have a plan." I concluded.

CHAPTER 37

We threw a plan together. We all understood that this plan, like all plans, would be good for as long as it lasted. No matter how well thought out and prepared, a plan seldom lasts past the first contact with the enemy. This plan had been made on the fly.

We decided to act based upon the opportunities presented. If the opportunity presented itself, we would take Nat Baha whenever, wherever. That was the plan.

If there wasn't a good way to get Baha at the concert venue, we would follow him to a better location. We compared notes on surveillance of a moving subject. Between the five of us we had three vehicles, the Tahoe, my truck and another, older SUV that David drove. For communication, we only had handheld radios and our cell phones.

I jumped in with David and he drove me over to the public access parking lot where my truck was parked. I jumped in my truck and followed him back to the gate of the secure parking area. Benjamin was there waiting to let us in. Somehow, the parking guard had been replaced or his shift was over.

I left my truck parked just inside the gate. The plan was, if we were forced to follow Baha, then Hafsah and I would leave ahead of him in my truck, with the others following from behind. Baha would be boxed in and we could stop him quickly if an opportunity presented itself. We would rotate positions as the situation dictated.

I called Tony and told him Hafsah and I were still at the concert venue and wouldn't be able to meet them at the restaurant after all. Tony was disappointed and I could tell he was curious about why we were still at the auditorium. I didn't volunteer any information, but I did promise to tell him all about it after church the next morning.

Back at the Tahoe, Hafsah had pulled out the black duffle bag. She now wore the black shoulder holster, under a dark blue windbreaker type jacket. The others had already seen to their armament from other stores they had brought with them. Hafsah sent me to put the black duffle bag in the cab of my truck. While I was doing that, the concert ended.

When I got back to the Tahoe, the decision had been made that three of us would go to the back of the building to see what might be done, as people came out the back door. Hafsah, David and I were to watch for any opportunity to grab or kill Baha. The other two would each have vehicles running and ready to go if we came back in a hurry.

We loitered in the general area, pretending to smoke cigarettes. Hafsah sent David up on the loading dock. She would signal him when Baha came out.

It was only a moment later when the steel door went up. By then, most of the crowd was swarming around the main public parking area. Men with handtrucks and dollies began bringing equipment out onto the loading dock. Several people, who worked in the venue came out of the building individually and in small clusters. Some went straight out to the secure parking area, got in their vehicles and drove away, while others hung out and socialized.

Shortly, there were half a dozen men working on the dock, putting things into the back of the trucks, as another half dozen moved back and forth, freighting the equipment from inside. There was no sign of anyone associated with the Honky Tonk Broncs. The rental truck stayed closed up. People who weren't working left the dock for the parking area.

David drifted away from the loading dock as soon as it started getting crowded.

I resisted the temptation to go back inside the building. I figured there was probably a great deal of activity going on in there as the venue was being cleaned, the stage and props were cleared, and some socializing and partying would be going on. Nat Baha would have no patience for any of that. Still, there would be some necessity for him and the band to participate in photo taking and being friendly. I decided I shouldn't risk it. Once inside, my record company persona would be blown in about one minute.

The larger trucks were mostly loaded by the time Kyle Coltrane and some of the members of his band came out. Right behind them, all four of the Honky Tonk Broncs came out onto the loading dock. Kyle Coltrane took a minute to talk to the roadies and shake hands all around, then he and his crowd headed for the buses. The Broncs stayed on the loading dock. Two more men came out with some equipment on dollies, and all of them started loading things into the back of their rental truck. They waved off any assistance from the other men who had loaded Kyle Coltrane's trucks.

The area on and around the loading dock was well lit, but it was not well lit where we were loitering out of sight to the men on the dock.

The men who loaded Coltrane's trucks went back inside.

"I could probably shoot Muktallah from here." David hissed at Hafsah, appearing suddenly beside us.

Just then, several of the roadies, stage hands and

some of the crew came out on the dock, laughing loudly. They were drinking beer in cans and bottles and smoking. They exchanged some jovial words with the men at the back of the truck.

Abdul Suliman and Jahander Khalid, appeared at the front of the truck, looking around. They both got in the cab, Khalid in the driver's seat. The truck started up and pulled away from the loading dock. Some of the men who had just come outside were still on the loading dock, but there was no sign of the four musicians! Where was the band? Had they gone back inside the auditorium?

Someone had to follow the truck. Someone had to go inside.

"David, you know what he looks like. Go inside and search quickly. We will follow the truck. Benjamin will be here if you need him. Call us as soon as you know if Muktallah is in the building" Hafsah made the decision quickly.

We sprinted over to the Tahoe where Anke was waiting with the engine running.

"Follow that truck," Hafsah instructed her. "We will be right behind you."

As Anke pulled out behind the truck, we ran over to Benjamin where he was seated in the other SUV.

"We lost Muktallah and the others. They may be inside the building, or they may be in the truck that just left. David has gone inside the building. You stay here and wait for him. Call us if there is trouble." She told him.

He nodded and held up his radio.

We ran to my truck, dived in and started it up. I had seen the taillights of the Tahoe as they disappeared toward the highway somewhere off to our right.

As we left the lot, I was thinking about how fast things can change. We had been forced to divide our team and we had no firm idea where Muktallah might be.

"So much for planning," I mumbled.

CHAPTER 38

Anke radioed she had the truck in sight and they were headed west on highway 64, towards the city. We stayed in communication for about five minutes until I turned north on loop 323 and spotted the Tahoe and the truck several car lengths ahead of us. We followed it to the cutoff for highway 271.

Hafsah's phone rang.

"Hello, David?" She listened to him talk for a moment. "There is nothing we can do. He has given us the slip. You and Benjamin should go on to the hotel. We are still following the truck." She paused to listen again. "No. There is no blame to assign. We will find him again, sooner or later. Goodbye."

Hafsah sighed and looked up through the moon roof of my truck.

"What is it?" I asked.

"We missed him at the auditorium. He and Aaron Parviz went back into the building. The other two members of the band are presumably in the back of the rental truck. David had not been inside the building and he became somewhat disoriented, with all of the hallways, searching room by room. He eventually asked someone if they had seen Nat Baha and Aaron Parviz. He was told they had gone out the front of the building to meet an Uber driver.

By the time he got to the front of the building the car was gone. David called Benjamin to come pick him up at the front of the building. I have sent them back to the hotel. Should we even continue to follow the rental truck?" She asked, clearly frustrated.

"Yes. It could be going to the same place the Uber driver is headed." I affirmed. "Tell Anke to drop back and we'll move up closer to the truck."

Two minutes later, the truck turned off of highway 271, into a public storage area with a high security fence around it.

We drove past it and did a u-turn at the next gap in the median. Anke stopped at the side of the road on the far side of the storage lot. We pulled into a parking lot directly across the highway.

Hafsah radioed Anke, who informed us she couldn't see the truck from where she was. I grabbed my binoculars and was watching the truck as Abdul Suliman and Jahander Khalid got out and went to the back. Suliman unlocked the door and slid it up. The bass player and the rhythm guitar player hopped down. They all stood and talked for a moment. Suliman pulled the door closed and locked it, as the two musicians walked over to where several vehicles were parked. They unlocked their individual vehicles and waved goodbye to Suliman and Khalid, who were also headed for their vehicles. Shortly, all four men drove out of the storage facility, the gate automatically shutting behind them. All four vehicles were headed back into town.

I was wondering why they hadn't unloaded the rental truck. Were they planning on hauling the equipment somewhere again soon?

This wasn't going well. Instead of three vehicles to run mobile surveillance on a single subject, we only had two vehicles to follow four subjects. There was little chance of success.

Moments later, even the little chance disappeared. The four vehicles split up; two continuing on into the city, the other two going in opposite directions on the loop. Hafsah radioed Anke and told her to head back to the hotel.

My phone rang.

"Hello, is this Mr. Hightower?" A familiar voice asked.

"You bet. Say, is that you, Mr. Baha?"

Hafsah and I looked at each other.

"It is, yes. Is this a bad time? I know you are dining with friends."

"Sure, we can talk."

"Are you still interested in doing a recording of our band?"

"I sure am. I have to say I'm particularly interested in you, though. You pretty much make the band what it is."

"You are too kind."

"So, Monday morning, I'll be at the recording studio. We need to sit down and talk details. We can do a demo whenever you and the band can get together. Before we get too far along, there are certain legal contract negotiations to be considered. I'm not asking for a contract right now, but we need to talk about these things."

"That discussion can be arranged. Mr. Parviz is our manager. He is here with me, as we speak."

"Excellent. I'll tell you what I'll do for you. On Monday, I'll provide the studio space and time. We'll do some sound checks and get something recorded at no expense to you. We'll just do a single which you can shop around if you want to. Naturally, I'd sure like you boys to sign with me, but I'll arrange this studio session. Call it a show of good faith."

"That is very generous, Mr. Hightower. It is what we would like to do."

"How about we meet first thing Monday morning, Mr. Baha?"

"… After morning prayer, Mr. Hightower."

"What? Oh, do you go to church on Monday?"

"It is our custom to pray in observance of salah, five times each day."

"Did you say salad? What does salad have to do with anything?"

"Really, Mr. Hightower, you have much to learn if you want to have any business with us. As Muslims, we observe the five pillars of Islam. One of these is daily prayer."

"OK, sure, I got no problem with that."

"An open mind is a virtue and the beginning of wisdom, Mr. Hightower. Perhaps you will begin to see the light. The candle is not there to illuminate itself."

"Huh?"

There was a moment of silence as Nat Baha regained his patience. I could almost feel his irritation vibrating through the truck's speakers.

"Monday will be fine, Mr. Hightower. Would nine o'clock be acceptable?"

"OK, that's fine. Do you know where the Superior Sound Systems studio is?"

"I am confident we can find it."

"Super! Nine AM, I'll look forward to seeing you then." I said.

He broke the connection.

"John, why do you play at being ignorant with my cousin?" Hafsah asked.

"Because he believes a typical American is ignorant, especially about Islam." I replied.

"Are most Americans ignorant about Islam?" she asked.

"Some are. Many believe Islam is just a religion, a matter of personal belief. There are not enough people who understand Islam is much more than a person's personal religion. In America we are a post Christian culture. In much of the country people have little exposure to any religion at all. There are too many people who think all religions are basically the same, useless and stupid. Few understand that for a person who is a fundamentalist Muslim, an Islamist, advancing the cause of Islam must be the most important aspect of their life.

Many Americans can't understand the concepts of jihad or martyrdom. There are more than two billion Muslims in the world. If ninety percent of them are peaceful, only about twenty million want to kill us. If a small fraction of those are committed to jihad… Most Americans can't imagine there are tens of thousands of people all over the world, many here in our country, who believe America is evil and worthy of destruction. They can't understand why those people would gladly give their lives in the process of taking ours. In this country we try to be respectful of other people's beliefs. We find it hard to believe other people don't hold the same view."

"How is this possible? Have they forgotten what happened on 9/11 in 2001?"

"No, Hafsah, they remember, but they think there are only a few crazy people who want to kill Americans. Until recently they thought those people were all in the Middle East and belonged to Al Qaeda or ISIS or another radical group. They don't understand how an otherwise intelligent and rational person living in America could decide to bomb a marathon or shoot up a group of people. They are ignorant about Islam in that way."

"Is Christianity really any different from Islam?" She asked.

"Oh yes, Hafsah, fundamentally different. Christians believe God sent His only son into the world, not to condemn the world, but so that the world might be saved. Christians believe God so loved the world, He gave His only begotten son, so that whoever believes in Him will be saved. Christians believe all people should have the chance to hear this message and make their own choices. Christians believe all people have free will and are responsible for the consequences of the choices they make. Christians don't judge or punish people who reject the gospel. Christians believe God alone is the final judge.

This differs from Islam, in that Islam believes

all people must worship Allah, even if they must be forced to do so. Islam teaches, any infidel who will not renounce their religion in favor of Islam is worthy of death. Islamists believe the entire world must be brought into subjugation to Islam, by any means necessary. Correct me if I'm wrong."

"You are not wrong John, but you are overlooking much of the teaching of the Prophet."

"Anyone truly committed to Islam would say a person who claims to be a Muslim but does not believe all of those things I just mentioned, has themselves overlooked much of the teaching and the example of the Prophet. Am I right?"

Hafsah nodded her head. In the glow of the truck's instruments, she looked very sad. "This is why there are so many radicals. But you Christians have done the same cruel things. What about the Crusades and the Inquisitions?"

"The Crusades were a reaction to the spread of Islam throughout the Middle East and spreading into Europe. It's true there were horrible atrocities committed, especially against the Jews. Those events occurred centuries ago when much of the world was under the thumb of the Roman Catholic Church. The crusades and inquisitions were the work of the Roman Catholic Church, not of all Christians. The Roman Catholic Church claimed to be the only true church. This is what happens when any group of people band together and decide only they have the truth, and then they decide whatever they say, that is the whole and only truth. The Roman Catholic Church attained political power. Power and corruption are intimate lovers. That's what the Inquisitions were all about. To maintain control, the Roman Catholic Church had to punish anyone who wouldn't toe the line. In this way, Islam and some churches are very much alike. The traditions and dogma become more important than the Word of God. That's not what Christianity is about.

As you know, every man-made religion or denomination is full of people who are members of the group, but it doesn't mean they are actually committed believers. Some people just want to belong to the group. Belonging to the Elks club doesn't make you an elk. Being born in a taxi doesn't make you a car. Being born into a Catholic or Protestant family doesn't make you a Christian. You were born to a Muslim father, but you were never really a Muslim. Many people call themselves Christians, but have no real idea what it means."

"I do not understand what you are saying." Hafsah said.

"I'm trying to describe the difference between adherence to a group and its traditions, and having a personal, living relationship with God."

"I would like that, John. I see how you trust and believe in God. I see how you love people. I hear how you pray, how you talk to God as though he were your father, and how you try to listen and obey. I want that in my life, John."

"Are you ready to meet Jesus?"

"Yes, I am."

I pulled the truck over to the side of the road.

We make our plans, but God has plans of His own.

Tonight, Hafsah had been forced to give up the chase in her attempt to capture her cousin. Instead, the hound of heaven had brought her to bay.

CHAPTER 39

As she climbed into bed, images and events of the day bounced and rolled in her mind like an old film shown from the wobbly reel of an unreliable projector.

Hafsah was exhausted, physically, mentally and emotionally.

She remembered how delightful it was walking hand in hand with John at the zoo. They strolled and enjoyed each other's company as if they didn't have a care in the world. There was no denying it — she was falling in love with him. Still, the man was infuriating. The concert had been fun, for a moment, until she realized who the lead guitar player was. She had been ready to kill Nat Baha in that moment, but was denied the satisfaction by the very circumstances that had put them together in the same time and place. Later, she found herself standing no more than eight feet from her hated cousin. She could have done it. The opportunity to be in the same room with him again might never come, but John had stopped her. Of course, there were witnesses and civilians in the room, but oh how she had wanted to pull the Glock from her purse and shoot the man, then and there.

That wasn't the last straw. John's constant reminders of her promise and her limitations had to stop. This man was her employee, not her boss! Yes, she was in love with him, but he was interfering with her mission. She had tried to walk away from John, but he wouldn't let her go. She thought she had fired him, but he didn't seem to notice. He held her to her promise, even as he held her heart.

When she had introduced John to her team, he practically took command. Anke's usually razor honed instincts and rock like dedication to a mission had been immediately overwhelmed. Did the man have the same effect on all women? Of course not, it was something else. Maybe it was the natural leadership he seemed to exude, or the thoughtful way he made his case for waiting to take Baha. Whatever it was, she had never seen her team take to an outsider so quickly.

Then there had been the fruitless and frustrating surveillance of the wrong suspects in the wrong vehicles. Nat Baha slipped away, as though he had planned it that way. So close, now he was gone again.

This had been without any question the most extraordinary day of her life. Her joys, sorrows, frustrations, fears and anxiety all culminating in a moment as she sat in the passenger seat of John's truck, late at night. He had introduced her to the man of her dreams. Not himself, but the man who had been born of a virgin, suffered as an innocent, died a martyr and rose from the dead in glory. Jesus, the Christ. John Wesley Tucker had introduced her to the messiah! She knew her life would never be the same.

How had all this happened? She had come to Texas to find and kill an international terrorist. It was the kind of mission at which she and her team had become proficient. From the moment she met John Wesley Tucker, the wheels had come off. She wasn't in control, she was in trouble. Even as Hafsah recognized this fact, she also realized how delightfully happy she was!

Slowly, Hafsah drifted off to sleep with a smile on her face and the most warm and peaceful feeling she had ever known.

CHAPTER 40

Christine and Tony met us at church the next morning.

Hafsah immediately spotted the sparkling diamond on Christine's finger.

"Oh, Christine that is a beautiful engagement ring!"

"It should be, it cost an arm and a leg." Tony said.

Christine gave him a gentle swat.

"… Her price is far above rubies" I quoted from Proverbs 31.

"Indeed, it is." Tony said.

Christine shot him a dirty look.

"What? I'm just agreeing with J.W." Tony said. "I've never known a more virtuous woman."

"Quit, while you're ahead." I advised him.

Tony changed the subject.

"Hafsah, I'm delighted to see you here. I don't mean to be rude, but last night you were wearing traditional Muslim clothing. Today, you look like the cover of Vogue magazine. Both are beautiful, but why so different?"

Hafsah smiled and said, "That was very tactful, Lieutenant Escalante."

"You haven't answered the question, and please call me Tony."

"Thank you, I will, Tony."

Tony looked at me.

"Is she always this evasive, J.W.?"

"Do you ever stop being a detective, Lieutenant Escalante?"

"It's a woman's right to wear whatever she wants." Christine cut in. "At least here in America, it is."

Tony looked confused.

Hafsah came to his rescue.

"Last night I was meeting some Muslim men. It was important they think of me as a traditional Muslim woman. Today I am a Christian. Do you understand, Tony?"

Tony was attempting to decipher what she was implying.

"Sure, I guess. When in Rome…"

"No, Tony. That's only part of what she's saying. Hafsah was raised as a Muslim. Since you saw her last night, there is a difference. Hafsah really has become a Christian." I said.

"Oh, that's wonderful news. We're sisters in Christ, Hafsah!" Christine exclaimed.

The two women hugged for a moment.

For a change, Tony was speechless.

After church we all went to lunch together at Liang's, our favorite Chinese restaurant.

I raised my water glass in a toast.

"I'm sorry we weren't able to join you last night, but I want to take this opportunity to toast the newly engaged."

The others raised their glasses.

"Tony, Christine, may God richly bless you in your marriage. May He draw you ever closer to Him and to each other."

"Hear, hear." Was the general response, as we clinked glasses all round.

Hafsah looked a little bemused.

"Is something wrong?" I asked her.

"Is it not considered bad luck to toast with water?" She asked.

"Yes, it is in some circles. When I was in the Navy, it was considered bad luck. I suppose somebody somewhere really believes if you step on a crack; it will cause the fracture of your mother's vertebrae. Or a broken mirror will bring seven years of bad luck. What is luck? I don't believe in luck, or silly superstitions. I believe God loves me and has good plans for my life. My concern needs to be following where He leads and obeying His word. If I'm doing that, I can break seven mirrors and walk on cracks all day long."

"Amen to that!" Tony said. "The toast is intended to bring people together in agreement on a special occasion. It shouldn't matter what the beverage is."

"We do it because we're celebrating a shared value."

"... Even though we're living in a country that's allowed the culture to dictate people's attitudes and values. What was once normal is now strange. What was weird is now normal. It's upside down and backwards." Christine added.

Hafsah nodded, and said, "I have seen what you are speaking of in many places throughout the world. Islam is a partial exception. Islam dictates what people's attitudes and values are to be, through the laws of sharia. In some countries this is strictly enforced, in others there is more tolerance of local cultural norms, is this not true of Christianity, as well."

"I understand what you're saying, but there is a difference. Where Islam dictates culture, Christianity informs culture. Where Islam enforces sharia, Christianity enforces nothing, allowing people to make their own choices, forgiving those who offend." Tony replied.

"Is there not much animosity between Christians, homosexuals, and people who have other alternative lifestyles? I have seen and heard reporting of how Christians are intolerant of many people in this culture." Hafsah said.

"Christians are supposed to recognize and address the sin in their own lives before they speak about anyone else's sin. Christians are just as guilty of sin as anyone else. The difference is Christians are striving to put an end to their own sinful habits. Christians are portrayed as being intolerant of other people's personal choices and private behavior. Christians tend to be intolerant of what they see as ever-increasing moral decay. There's conflict, because some of the most sinful behaviors in this culture are flaunted and glorified. Christians would never celebrate their own shameful sin and flaunt it publicly. We can't celebrate our shame.

Until very recently that was a shared value in our culture. Christians are opposed to public policy and open displays of behavior that's contrary to the teachings of the scriptures. This is viewed as being intolerant of the people themselves. Saying anything in opposition to this celebration of sin and moral decay of the culture is considered hate speech in many parts of the country. If it's any form of intolerance, it's intolerance of being forced to support something we believe is wrong. When the Supreme court announced that homosexual marriage should become the law of the land, some people celebrated, others mourned. There were judges, justices of the peace, and county clerks all across the country, who felt they had to resign their positions because they couldn't bring themselves to sanction something they believed was wrong. Many of them were publicly castigated and ridiculed." Tony said.

Hafsah considered his answer.

"The definition of what we call 'culture' is formed by people's shared attitudes and values. It represents the behavioral norm of a group of people or a society. Christine's point is that the present culture strives to get all people to reject everything we used to have as shared traditional attitudes and values, and replace them with personal and individualized values. What happens when everyone is pretty much free to do whatever they want? It's the very thing that causes division, insecurity and eventually, lawlessness. We're seeing lawlessness spreading across the country. There are more and more people with no respect for law and order. This emphasis on individual liberty, without shared or common values, creates conflicts and eventually destroys a culture." I said.

"America has exported many cultural elements to other parts of the world, everything from fast food to hip-hop music and pornography. I suspect personal freedom and rejection of traditional values is also part of the culture we export." Tony suggested.

"It is one of the reasons Islam hates the west. Islamic leaders see the west as corrupt and vile. In many respects, I think they are right." Hafsah said.

We all considered her statement for a moment.

"Culture tries, but fails, to dictate what the people of God do. I'm reminded of Daniel, Shadrach, Meshach and Abednego. They were dragged away from Israel and taken into a completely different culture in Babylon. They refused to bow to those edicts that violated the Law of Moses or the leading of God." I said. "They lived as people of faith in the midst of a culture opposed to those values."

"Right, whatever the cultural norm may be, there are people within the culture who have differing values. He mentioned Daniel and his friends, back in the day. A more modern example is the Amish people here in America. Because of their beliefs they've rejected much of the modern, mechanized and digital world. They continue to live, or at least try to live, in the same way their ancestors did, sharing common values. So devoted to those values, they're still plowing with horses and lighting their homes with lamps and candles, while you and I are ordering smart phones off the internet." Tony said.

"Good example. To me, it proves people can hold on to their personal beliefs and values in the midst of a world that's becoming increasingly contrary and counter to those beliefs and values." I said.

"Can one do both? Can a person accept and enjoy the things of the world and remain devoted to their faith?" Hafsah asked.

"The Bible says, 'Do not love the world or the things in the world. If anyone loves the world, love for the Father is not in him. For all that is in the world, the lust of the flesh, the lust of the eyes and the pride of life, is not of the Father, but is of the world. And the world passes away, and the lust of it; but he who does the will of God abides forever'." I quoted. "Christians struggle every day to overcome the temptations and distractions of the world, the flesh, and the devil. We live in the world, but we are not of the world. We can enjoy some of the things of the world, but we cannot love those things. We are called to be salt and light for the world. So, we inform and model what it means to be a Christian. We hold to the values we've learned and let our light shine in the darkness. We must bloom where we're planted, even in the midst of a hostile environment." I said.

"Is this not an example of why Christians must strive to maintain their commitment to their core beliefs in the midst of a changing culture?" Hafsah asked.

"It is," I said. "The culture is becoming more and more hostile towards Christians, who are viewed by many as backwards or even mentally deficient. The number of people who self-identify as Christian is dwindling in this country."

"… At least for now." Christine observed. "Let's not worry about all that. Each day is a gift. Yesterday is a memory and tomorrow is a mystery. We only have today. I'm glad we all get to spend some time together, today."

"This is the day the Lord has made, let us rejoice and be glad in it." I quoted.

"Well, amen to that, too!" Tony replied.

"Yep, today is a great day, congratulations again, you two." I said. I raised my glass in their honor.

I hold that moment in my mind, like a snapshot in a photo album. The four of us sitting there, grinning at each other like we didn't have a care in the world.

CHAPTER 41

We heard sirens in the distance, not uncommon in a city of this size. Immediately there were multiple sirens as fire trucks and police cars headed West on the south loop raced by, right outside the restaurant.

"I wonder what all that's about…" I started to say.

Tony's pager and his cell phone both chirped at the same time, interrupting me. He answered the phone, as he looked at his pager. He listened, his eyes got big and his mouth dropped open.

"…In route, ETA three minutes. Scramble SWAT and request assistance from all available officers in all agencies." He said into the phone, as he leaped up from the table.

"I have to go. There's an active shooting incident at the mall. J.W., will you and Hafsah take Christine home, please." He gave Christine a quick squeeze and a peck on the cheek.

"Be safe…" Christine called to him as he ran for the exit.

Hafsah and I stared at each other for a moment, both of us thinking the same thought. "Let's go to the office." I suggested. I waived to the waitress to bring us our bill.

"I need to go to the hotel." Hafsah said.

"I think it might be better if you call your team, and invite them to join us at my office."

Christine was chewing her lip.

"Why? Do you two know what's happening?" She asked.

My office was only about three quarters of a mile and only two stop lights away from the restaurant. Oddly, it was about the same distance from the mall. The parking lot of the six-story office building was virtually abandoned on a Sunday. The bank occupying the first floor was closed and there was little or no business being conducted in any of the offices on the other floors.

When the three of us raced into my outer office, I turned on the television. There was nothing on the national news or the cable channels related to the current event. They were all still focused on the FBI raid in East Texas. What could have gone wrong? What was the real cause of the explosion at that remote farmhouse?

None of the network affiliates had news programs on at this time on a Sunday afternoon. The local news was trying to get on top of the story. A ticker popped up at the bottom of a football game on one channel, advising the public to avoid the area around the mall. Police had reported a shooting at the mall with an unknown number of casualties... On another channel a shaken news reporter appeared on the screen announcing they were breaking into the scheduled program to report there was some sort of shooting incident at the mall.

"Ladies and gentlemen, we are being told the public should avoid the area around Broadway and Loop 323. It seems there's been a shooting at the shopping mall on South Broadway at Loop 323, in the city of Tyler. Let me repeat this, the public is asked to avoid the area around the shopping mall on South Broadway at Loop 323, in Tyler. Witnesses have said they heard multiple gunshots inside the mall. The scene is chaotic and emergency vehicles are having difficulty getting through the traffic. Again, the public is advised to avoid the area around the mall located on South Broadway, in the city of Tyler. We'll continue to monitor the situation and bring you the story as fast as we can. This is an on-going situation and we have a reporter on the way to the scene. We return you now to the program already in progress."

"What do you think is happening, John?" Hafsah asked.

"It's too soon to tell. There have been other incidents and shootings at the mall. The place is popular with young people and some of them are in gangs. Sometimes things get out of hand."

I changed the channel.

"… I've heard it before. I'm telling you, I know an AK when I hear one. Two tours in Nam. I'll tell you something else. There was more than one shooter. People were screaming…"

A reporter was interviewing someone on the scene.

Now we knew. There was only one logical conclusion.

Jihadist butchers had attacked the mall. The feds had seen something coming, but not in time to stop it. We were also responsible. The bloodshed and loss of life was partially due to our own failure.

Within hours, every major news organization in the United States was on the scene and Tyler was once again on the map. This was the top story and would be the banner headline on Monday morning in every newspaper in the country. No other story could be as riveting or good for their ratings. Acts of terrorism and mass murders of the general public were much more interesting to see being discussed by the talking heads on the morning television news programs.

The rest of the afternoon was filled with watching the news and discussing what, when, and if we could do anything to put an end to this horror. Christine was no longer afforded the privilege of ignorance. Initially her primary concern was for Tony's safety.

That concern was replaced by outrage and anger. She became part of the discussion of what could be done to find and stop these killers.

After her team joined us, Hafsah spoke with her superiors in Israel. It was being discussed in Israel whether or not, and to what degree to alert the FBI and provide them with the information we had gathered. For now, Hafsah and her team were ordered to continue gathering intelligence and be prepared to act if the opportunity presented itself.

I was ready to hand the whole thing over to Jack and the federal authorities. I was even tempted to call Tony and tell him the whole story. Failure to provide law enforcement authorities with information would probably be construed as interference in a criminal investigation and could get me arrested. I had no desire to be considered any kind of an accomplice to this madness. On the other hand, the feds knew all about it, long before I did.

As we discussed it, we agreed the only thing we actually knew or could tell the authorities was who and what we suspected. We had the names of some people we suspected. It was information the feds already had. In fact, we got our information from the DHS through Jack. The various federal agencies probably had more information than we did. We had no idea where any of the suspects were, or if they were even actually involved in this diabolical nightmare. Mossad made it very clear any information provided to the federal authorities was to come from Israel through diplomatic channels, and not from any of us. Evidently, they assumed I was somehow answerable to Mossad.

As the afternoon wore on, it became apparent there were multiple fatalities and countless wounded. We learned both hospitals had been overwhelmed with wounded, many of whom were flown to Dallas.

There were several dozen police officers on the scene from several different agencies. As the lead investigator and the senior officer of the Robbery/ Homicide division of the Tyler police department, Tony would be coordinating all of the various departments and agencies involved. A tactical team would have to be sent into the mall. Every nook and cranny had to be searched for the gunmen, the dead and wounded, and those who had hidden themselves from the gunmen. This seemed to take hours. Eventually it was reported the mall was secured.

The news media became inundated with new information, rumors and witnesses. They reported there were at least three gunmen who opened fire inside the mall as they raced from one end to the other. A general panic ensued as people tried to run away or hide. It was possible there had been armed citizens in the mall exchanging gunfire with the shooters. Consequently, there were widely varied descriptions of the number of shooters and what they looked like. From the wide-ranging descriptions, about all that could be learned was that the witnesses seemed to agree the gunmen had been males of medium height, wearing dark colored pants and a variety of outerwear. They wore ski masks, so no one saw their faces. The entire shooting rampage had lasted less than four minutes from the time the first shots were fired. Most of the casualties had occurred at the south end of the mall, where the shooting started. As they ran north, the gunmen hadn't taken the time to enter any of the stores, only firing into them when they saw targets as they ran past. They shot anyone they encountered in the central walkway or attempting to escape into the stores. It was already estimated that hundreds of rounds had been fired. The mall was a disaster area. Several witnesses reported hearing the men screaming "Allahu Akbar" as they sprayed the mall with gunfire. The gunmen had escaped and were at large.

The city was in shock.

The investigation of the shooting itself would go on for days. Every frame of video from the security cameras would be enhanced and analyzed. All cell phone images that might have recorded anything useful would undergo the same scrutiny. Every inch of the interior of the mall would be examined for evidence. Each shell casing would be collected and analyzed. All shots fired and bullet trajectories would be recreated. Every person in the mall that day and witnesses outside would undergo skilled interrogation, including those victims who survived. The entire event would be re-enacted moment by moment, shot by shot.

A simultaneous investigation to identify and find the shooters would take an unknown amount of time. Time the shooters would use to their advantage, time to disappear, time to prepare the next attack.

The clock was ticking.

It was a mercy the shooting had happened on a Sunday after noon. Had it been a Saturday or during a holiday shopping season, the death toll would have been much higher.

I was reminded of the purpose of this terrorist act. Terror was the goal. The number of people killed or wounded was not the goal. Killing was simply necessary to terrorize the population. Terrorizing the entire region had been achieved with a little over three minutes of gunfire, on a Sunday afternoon. This was just the first act of many to follow and other jihadists were out there somewhere, watching and planning their own assaults in their own regions of the country.

If we didn't stop it here, we wouldn't stop it anywhere.

By suppertime, we learned that among the dead were two Tyler police officers who had been on duty at the sub-station. An off duty cop had been killed outside the Victoria's Secret shop. A security guard, three children and more than a dozen other people had been shot to death. There would be others who would die in hospital. From previous experience we knew that eventually the whole world would learn the names and stories of each person who had fallen.

Somewhere near the center of all that havoc was a man with credentials that said United States Department of Homeland Security. Jack had his hands full now.

If only I could trust him.

Based on witness statements and video imagery, the public was told to be on the lookout for a silver colored, or possibly grey, Toyota minivan of indeterminate age, a blue Chevrolet sedan, a white SUV, A white, four door Dodge pickup, etc. No license numbers were given. It was clear the police didn't know for sure what the escaped gunmen may have been driving. At any given time on a typical Sunday afternoon, a dozen or more different vehicles could be leaving the mall, any of which could've held one or all of the gunmen. The shooting prompted a mass exodus form the parking lots surrounding the mall. Witness accounts were conflicting and generally unreliable. Eventually it would be narrowed down and more clearly stated. Eventually would be far too late. The escape vehicles would be found abandoned and burned. The gunmen would have disappeared out in the piney woods somewhere, into the secure hideout previously prepared. Maybe even the very place Nat Baha had been living and training the gunmen since he arrived in East Texas.

We all understood there was very little chance we would ever see any of the gunmen until they struck again.

Only one hope remained. It was the thinnest of possibilities.

Would Nat Baha and the Honky Tonk Broncs band take the bait and show up at the recording studio?

Could he be that egotistical?

CHAPTER 42

As usual, things had not gone exactly as planned.

Driving the stolen minivan, Nat Baha dropped the three men off at the south end of the mall. He drove around to the north end and parked. Leaving the engine running he checked his watch. It had taken him nearly two and a half minutes to drive the distance. That left about two minutes for the men to emerge from Penny's and jump into the minivan. He rolled down the windows and immediately heard the sounds of muffled gunfire.

In front of him people began running out of the store, a woman could be heard screaming. He saw people running out into the car park area on the east side of the mall. From where he was parked he couldn't see anything on the west side, but he figured it would be the same way, panic and chaos, as people fled for their lives.

He checked his watch again. One minute to go. Just then he saw Jahander Khalid stumble out of Penny's. He was clearly wounded, perhaps badly so. A second later, Aaron Parviz limped out. It was evident he was wounded as well. Abdul Suliman backed out the doors, spraying bullets back into the building. He spun around and helped Aaron Parviz catch Khalid as he fell.

Gunning the engine Baha brought the car up in front of the men. Suliman opened the sliding door and shoved Khalid onto the floor board. Parviz clamored painfully inside. Suliman leapt in and slid the door closed as Nat Baha pulled away from the front of the store.

There were already other cars trying to leave the parking lot. More people were running through the lot trying to get to their cars. The terror and panic spreading outward from the mall in waves. Baha pulled in behind a couple of vehicles and prayed for them to get out of the way.

"What happened? Is Khalid alright?"

"Shit! It all went to shit." Suliman said, trying to help Khalid. "It started exactly as we planned. We shot a bunch of people on the south side, and kept moving north. We shot cops and civilians alike. They were like sitting ducks. By the time we got to the central courtyard, some people were already escaping through the front entrance. We let them go and continued north past all those little kiosks, firing into the stores. That's where we ran into trouble. By then some armed men had found cover and opened up on us as we went past them. We had to make a running fight. We took out more people… Shit! He's dead. I think Khalid's dead, man." He tore off his ski mask.

"Calm down." Nat Baha said, focused on getting on the road, he made a right turn out onto South Broadway. "Aaron, how badly are you injured?"

"I don't know. I think I'll be OK. I took one in the leg and another through my side. I'm just afraid I'll bleed to death. Is Jahander really dead?"

Cars were now streaming out of all the parking lots. Sirens could be heard coming from every direction.

"Our brother has given his life in the cause of jihad. His place in Paradise is assured. Allahu Akbar! You have all performed well, Aaron. You have proven yourselves warriors of Islam."

Suliman turned his attention to Aaron's injuries. "You'll be OK. The leg wound still has a bullet in it. It's not bleeding too badly. The wound in your side missed anything vital, but it's a bleeder. I need to get some pressure on the exit wound. This is going to hurt."

After about ten minutes of crawling along with the traffic headed south on Broadway, it began to flow more normally. Five minutes later they were headed out into the country side. They had seen a lot of emergency vehicles headed for the mall, but none had shown any interest in them.

Nat Baha pulled into a church parking lot where a four-door pickup was parked. Sam Jones and Mohammad Hussien were waiting for them in the stolen vehicle. The two men helped move Aaron into the backseat of the pickup while Nat Baha shifted the assault rifles to the bed of the truck. He took a five-gallon container of a diesel and gasoline mixture from the truck and poured most of it over Jahander Khalid's body inside the minivan. He splashed the rest around liberally inside the vehicle, saving only enough to make a long trailing puddle away from the minivan. Lighting the puddle, he jumped into the pickup as it drove away. Seconds later the minivan erupted in a ball of flames.

CHAPTER 43

"It's not too late for him. He can still repent and choose redemption." I said.

Hafsah and I were sitting in her hotel room discussing the possibilities for the next day.

"My cousin is a murderer of the innocent. Their blood is on his hands. He is not fit to live." Hafsah replied.

"I agree, Hafsah. The thing is, you and I are not innocent of bloodshed either. We've done things for which we can be neither proud nor happy. We may not be murderers, but Jesus said whatever a person thinks and feels in his heart, is the sin of which he's guilty. Hate, lust, envy, murder, we have done all these sins in our hearts and minds. Even if we haven't committed the act, we are guilty of the attitude. God is rich in mercy. He has extended His mercy toward us 'in that while we were yet sinners, Christ died for us. If we confess our sins, He is faithful and just to forgive our sins and cleanse us from all unrighteousness'. I know it doesn't seem fair, but if your cousin will repent and call upon the name of the Lord, he can be saved."

"Where is the justice in that?" She asked.

"God is the Judge, Hafsah. He sets the rules and determines the final judgment. His justice does not negate His mercy, nor does His mercy negate His justice. There are consequences for the choices and actions we make and those your cousin has made. We all have to deal with those consequences. He will have to face those consequences, but his ultimate fate rests with God."

"I will not hesitate to kill him."

"If he must be killed to stop him from doing further harm, neither will I. But you must understand, I can't kill him if there is any chance, he will repent."

"If you hesitate, he will kill you."

"We've talked about this. My fate, like his, rests in the hands of God. I desire mercy for him, but I'm prepared to do justice. I must ask the same of you."

"Inch' Allah." Hafsah replied.

"Yes, if it is God's will. Will you pray with me about that?"

She nodded her head in silent agreement.

Later, as I was driving home, I considered what God might be doing in my life. Sometimes, He speaks so clearly, I know exactly what I must do. Often, trying to see His plan is like to trying to follow a trail of breadcrumbs in a snowstorm. The trail is there, but it is not easy to follow and any distraction can throw you off. The good news is that eventually the snow will melt and the trail will be more clearly seen. Sometimes it requires waiting for the weather to improve, even while we want to push on faster. Some start on the trail but give up when the going gets hard. Others wander around, going down whatever path they happen to find, hoping to stumble back on the correct trail at some later time. Only the person who has chosen to follow the appointed trail and stays committed to the journey will arrive at the intended destination. I've made my share of mistakes, following the wrong trails.

On this occasion, my relationship with Hafsah could alter the entire course of my mission on this planet. I couldn't afford to misinterpret the message. I was starting to have difficulty imagining my life without Hafsah by my side. Could that be the plan? Why would God put her in my life, only to take her away again?

Hafsah would be leaving soon. If we were able to capture or kill Nat Baha and his band of butchers, her assignment would be over. If we failed and they escaped, her assignment would take her somewhere else.

I didn't want her to ever go away. I was struggling with that knowledge. What did it mean? What could I do about it? Could I ask her to stay? If I did ask her, would she stay? Could she?

I would have to play the hand I was dealt.

The first order of business was setting the trap for Nat Baha. The plan was to capture him and whoever was with him, when and if they showed up at the studio the next morning.

The studio was an ideal place to trap the killers. We had determined there was only the main entrance and a single back door as routes of ingress and egress. Off the back hallway there was an office room with windows down one side and two restrooms with high narrow windows. The only other exterior windows in the building were the big picture windows that flanked the front doors. Most of the building was dedicated to recording and there were no exterior windows in those areas. The primary recording studio area had no exterior windows and it was sound proof.

We had enough manpower to cover all avenues of escape. Once the band entered the recording area, it would be easy to prevent them from leaving, at least leaving alive.

Christine and Anke would welcome them to the studio, and once the band was inside, they would guard the doorway to the front exit of the building, with weapons ready. Benjamin and David would be in the control room overlooking the recording studio. From there they could guard the hallway leading to the back door. That left Hafsah and me to confront Baha and the band in the recording studio proper. Surrounded, outnumbered and out gunned, Baha and his band would have to surrender. If it became a gunfight, Christine, Anke, Benjamin and David could catch them in crossfire from the doorways.

This was as good a plan as we could hope for. We would have them in a time and place of our choosing. A place where there would be no innocent bystanders endangered. A place designed to contain noise. Even fully automatic gunfire would not be heard outside the building.

It was the best we could do and it was out of our hands. Nat Baha and the boys would show up, or they wouldn't.

As the six of us had discussed the matter, we were generally agreed it would be highly unlikely the terrorists would abandon their hidey hole and venture back into Tyler. On the other hand, there was just the slightest chance they would think they had gotten away clean and no one suspected them.

It all came down to what Nat Baha believed. If he believed it was safe, he was pretty committed to getting a demo record cut, he might take the risk. If he believed it wasn't safe, he would have already headed for greener pastures, leaving the locals to take their chances in additional future raids.

I had an idea forming at the back of my mind.

Daylight would reveal all.

CHAPTER 44

In the darkness, Nat Baha walked around the safe house with only his thoughts for company.

As they had watched the local news coverage on an old boxy television, he and the others had spent the last hours of daylight patching up Aaron Parviz and discussing the attack, while cleaning their weapons, they had kicked around ideas about what might happen next.

His little band of musicians and fighters were all asleep now. He had chosen to take the first watch.

The mission had been a success. He and his mujahidin had brought the city to its knees. The entire world was learning what they had done. He had advanced jihad on America, and he had lost only one man in this first strike. Fortunately, it was not one of the musicians.

The television coverage suggested the government and police agencies had no idea who had committed the raid. In a day or two, he would declare victory on behalf of the Islamic State.

As he walked, he was considering his options. Initially, the plan was to hide out at the training camp until it was time to strike again. Recent events had altered that plan. The game warden stumbling on the property had been unexpected, but not unanticipated. Over the years, the angel had taught him to prepare for any eventuality. As soon as he arrived in this horribly humid place, he had put the locals to work finding suitable back up facilities and other secure locations. This modular house on five acres surrounded by dense forest was one of them.

It was so easy to do in America. No one cared who rented their property, as long as they weren't too seedy looking and had the required deposit. People didn't pay much attention to their neighbors. This was even more convenient in the deep woods. America truly was a land of liberty, including incredibly trouble-free traveling without any restriction. Transportation was abundant and the roads were excellent.

As he was thinking about these things, Nat Baha felt another presence in the night. He recognized it immediately. Gabriel had come to him. He stopped walking and quickly looked around, but he was still unable to see the angel. No matter, he was getting guidance from the unseen spirit being. He didn't have to see the angel in order to receive the instruction. He felt it within every fiber of his being.

Yes, of course. It was obvious to him now. There was no need for any of them to hide. On the contrary, the more open they were in their movements, the better it would be. The men should return to their normal activities until it was time to go on the road with the Kyle Coltrane concert tour. The tour would provide transportation to new, target rich, areas of the country. It would be, as he had told his mujahedeen, a perfect cover. The men should all return to their day to day lives until then. Everyone who knew them would expect them to be excited about the upcoming opportunity. They would spend the next couple of weeks getting ready for the tour.

Nat Baha smiled.

Before they went about the routine aspects of their lives, there was just one more thing he and the band needed to do.

CHAPTER 45

We were ready by eight o'clock the next morning. When we arrived at the studio, we immediately took it under our exclusive control. A great deal of money had been spent to assure we would be the only people present at the studio. Christine and Anke were at the front, Christine behind the reception desk. Benjamin and David were at the soundboards in the control room that overlooked the studio space. Hafsah and I were in the primary studio recording room. This was a huge room. It was set up to accommodate a number of musicians and do so with a certain amount of comfort.

In addition to the two huge sofas, on opposite walls, there were two electronic keyboards, a grand piano, two full drum sets, with a variety of additional percussion apparatus, various microphones and stands, amplifiers, speakers, stools, tables, and other equipment. The floor had cables snaking around, most of which were taped down. The walls were all covered in acoustic enhancing and sound dampening textured tiles. There were doors that opened into three smaller sound booths for recording individual vocal or instrumental performances.

Hafsah was dressed for whatever might happen. She wore the same outfit she had worn to the picnic, right down to the Glock in the shoulder holster. I found the slogan on her T-shirt ironic, 'just do it' was what we were hoping Nat Baha would decide. It might have a whole new meaning before the morning was over. We were all armed, locked and loaded, the fully automatic Uzis strategically hidden within easy reach.

None of us expected to see the murderous musician, but we had to be prepared in the event he did show up. We were resolved that if Nat Baha walked in, he wouldn't walk out.

We were all attuned to the ticking clock, counting the minutes as the appointed time approached.

At precisely nine o'clock, in walked Nat Baha. Aaron Parviz and Abdul Suliman followed right behind him. All three men were dressed casually. Aaron Parviz looked pale and he was limping prominently. Clearly his left leg had suffered an injury. He appeared to be in extreme pain and possibly drugged. There was no sign of Jahander Khalid.

"Good morning!" I called, as they came into the room.

"As-salamu alayka." Nat Baha replied gravely. He scowled a little as he eyed Hafsah in her western street clothes. He was carrying a guitar case in his left hand. Suliman had one in his left hand as well.

I saw Suliman studying Hafsah surreptitiously as he and Baha placed their guitar cases on one of the tables.

Aaron Parviz approached Hafsah.

"Why are you dressed that way, Nadia?" He asked thickly, clearly confused.

"Good morning gentlemen. May I offer you coffee or tea?" She replied, ignoring his comment.

"Thank you, no. Ms. Ahmed, isn't it?" Nat Baha asked her.

I wasn't comfortable with the laser like attention being focused on Hafsah and the direction this conversation was going. I decided to change it.

"Mr. Parviz, this is a great day for your band. Can I show you around? Say, you're injured. Will you be able to play the drums?"

Up close, I could see he was sweating. I was sure he was drugged, probably sedated and high on pain pills. Evidently, there had been an exchange of gunfire at some point in the carnage at the mall. Texans tend to be armed and these guys had been unprepared to have armed citizens shooting back at them. Whether it was an armed citizen, a cop, or a security guard didn't matter. Parviz had been hit, maybe more than once. Had something similar happened to Khalid?

"He will manage, Mr. Hightower." Nat Baha replied.

I figured he could. How many rock and roll musicians had played while they were stoned?

I turned my attention to the two men as they unlatched the guitar cases.

"I didn't get the name of your lead singer on the rhythm guitar. Will he be here soon?" I asked.

"His birth name was Robert Tolliver. Recently he has changed it to Mohammad Hussein. He will join us shortly." Nat Baha replied.

"And the bass player…?"

"… Sam Jones. He is with Mr. Hussein. As I said, they will be here shortly. This gentleman is Abdul Suliman. He is in charge of our equipment."

"Hey, Abdul," I said, shaking his hand.

"While we are waiting, perhaps you will show us around the studio, Mr. Hightower." Baha suggested.

"… Sure thing, Nat. Can I call you Nat? You can call me Earl."

"Very well, Earl."

"As you can see, this space is the primary recording studio. The domed ceiling is an innovative design to reduce the sound bouncing back down. The walls are covered in acoustic tile as one would expect, but even the floor is sound absorbent. If you drop a drumstick or knock over a stool, it won't ruin a recording. Listen… can you hear that…? That's the sound of complete silence, there's no ambient noise. The equipment in here is all primo, the best of the best. Every microphone and amplifier is connected to the control booth over there. Those guys you see in there are a couple of the best sound techs and mixers in the business. They'll make this recording sound the best it possibly can. Would you like to meet them and have a look at the boards?"

"I would be pleased." Nat Baha replied.

As I headed for the door to the control booth, I was concerned there were three missing members of the group, somewhere outside the building. I wasn't sure the men in the control booth had hidden their guns well enough. There was nothing I could do but stall for time.

I stopped and turned to Abdul Sulliman

"Don't you want to take a look at the sound boards, Abdul?"

"No, thank you. I wouldn't know what I was looking at. I just move and set up the band's stuff, wherever the gig is. I'm going out to the truck to get the rest of what we'll need."

"You won't need much. Everything in here is available for your use."

"Mr. Baha is particular about what equipment he uses." He replied.

I shrugged and turned to Aaron Parviz.

"Mr. Parviz, can I call you Aaron?"

"Yeah, Ok." He replied, dully.

"Aaron, that show the other night was sensational. Had you performed with Kyle Coltrane before?"

"Uh uh," He said, with a shake of his head.

"Mr Coltrane was very impressed with the audience response to our performance. He has invited the band to go on tour with him, as his opening act." Nat Baha informed me.

"Perfect! That's exactly the kind of exposure you boys need. With a demo record in hand you'll be all set to take L.A. or Nashville by storm."

"Inch'Allah, Mr. Hightower.

"Huh?"

"What happens or does not happen beyond this moment, is in the hands of Allah, may his name be forever praised and adored. We are but his servants."

"Oh, right, yeah, I get that. One thing at a time, today we make a demo record. When are you boys supposed to hit the road with Kyle Coltrane?

"The first of October. May we see the control room now?"

"Sure. Not a problem."

I opened the door to the control booth and stuck my head inside.

"Nat Baha and Aaron Parviz would like to take a look at the sound boards. Is that OK with you boys?" I asked.

Benjamin and David were both seated on rolling stools behind the sound boards, as though they knew what they were doing. Their Uzis were stashed out of sight.

They had adopted a kind of "who cares" attitude.

"Whatever, man." David said.

"We're ready whenever you are." Benjamin said, catching my eye.

"We'll get started shortly. We're waiting on a couple of the band members." I replied.

I stepped aside and indicated that Baha and Parviz should go on in.

"Might be a little crowded in there, but take a look." I said.

"As-salamu alayka." Nat Baha said to the men, as he entered the sound booth.

"Aleichem Shalom." David replied instinctively.

I froze.

"Your Hebrew is excellent, sir. Are you Israeli?" Nat Baha asked David.

My hand went inside my jacket.

"Nope, born and raised in Brooklyn. I'm David. Where are you from?" David asked casually.

"My name is Nat Baha. I was born in Spain." He offered a handshake.

"Cool." David said, shaking his hand, "I hear you're something else on lead guitar."

"I work at it, thanks be to Allah." Baha replied, "This is Aaron Parviz, the leader of the band."

"Howdy, boys, I'm Ben." Benjamin said.

"I must say, I am impressed with the quality of this equipment." Baha observed.

"It'll do the job, man." David agreed.

I began to relax. David and Benjamin were professionals. They had handled David's slip as if it were the most natural thing in the world.

"Time is money, boys. Let's get you set up. Maybe the others will wander in while we're doing it." I suggested.

"As you say, Earl, I will send them a text message and encourage them to come along. They have their instruments with them." He took out his cell phone and began tapping out a note.

CHAPTER 46

In preparation for a recording we had no idea how to make, nor any intention of making, we began setting up microphones, guitar stands and other gear, checking the wiring connections. Christine was photographing the whole process. I thought it was a nice touch, as though this was a historic event. The first recording session would be an important moment for the band. Abdul Suliman came back in with equipment stacked on a hand-truck. There were a couple more guitar cases. He began unloading these things next to the table where the other guitar cases were placed.

As we were doing these things, Mohammad Hussein, formerly known as Robert Tolliver, came in with Sam Jones. They had their own guitar cases, which they placed on the same table with the others. We made the usual introductions.

There was no sign of Jahander Khalid. Where was he? I didn't like having anyone unaccounted for, but I couldn't exactly ask where he was.

The show must go on.

We had two microphones on stands for the vocalists, additional microphones to pick up the full sound of the band, and another pair just for the drum set. The guitars would be hooked up to amplifiers and the feed from all of the microphones and amps would also go directly into the control room. Speakers in the studio would send the sound back into the room as a track was being laid down. Once an initial recording was captured the sound would be sent back into the room for the approval of the musicians. At least that was what was supposed to happen.

Aaron Parviz took a seat behind the drums and picked up his drumsticks.

Mohammad Hussein stepped up to a microphone.

"Check, check, 1,2,3,4, check, check." He said into the microphone. There was no sound coming from any of the speakers. He looked at the switch on the microphone. He looked over at the sound booth, flicking the switch.

David and Benjamin were staring at us, unaware they were supposed to be monitoring and adjusting sound levels.

Mohammad Hussein waved at the sound booth and pointed at the microphone and then at his own ears, signaling that the microphone was not turned on.

In the sound booth, I saw Benjamin and David both scrambling to figure out how to turn it on.

Nat Baha was getting one of his guitars out of a case. He was watching the confusion in the booth. Abdul Suliman was opening a case and speaking quietly to him. Nat Baha glanced at Hafsah.

That was all the warning I had.

Several horrible things happened at once.

What Nat Baha pulled out of the guitar case wasn't a Stratocaster, but an AK 47. He swung toward Hafsah, opening fire.

Hafsah pulled her Glock free of the shoulder holster as the first bullet hit her, half turning her.

I found Nat Baha in the front site of my .45 and fired four shots. Swinging over on Abdul Suliman, who had pulled another AK and had started firing at the sound booth, I fired my last three rounds and ejected the magazine.

Anke and Christine ducked in from the front hallway, selecting targets and firing as they came through the doorway. Anke came in low holding an Uzi, firing in short controlled bursts. Christine followed Anke, firing the Judge revolver I had given her a year or so before.

Mohammad Hussein, and Sam Jones had both pulled handguns and were caught off guard by the sudden appearance of the two women. They had intended to shoot me, but had to turn toward the women.

I slapped another magazine into my .45, as Benjamin and David reappeared from behind the soundboard where they had been forced to duck as the hail of bullets and broken glass had flown into the booth. They both opened up with their Uzis on Hussein and Tolliver.

Those men were shot to pieces in the crossfire from the women and the men in the control booth.

The nearly perfect acoustics of the recording studio allowed us all to hear the roar of the gunfire with particular clarity. The total silence that immediately followed the exchange made me think for a moment I had gone deaf.

I could see Nat Baha was down, but Suliman was hidden from my sight by the table and stack of equipment.

I spun to get a look at Hafsah.

She was down.

Still sitting behind the drums, unmoved and unmoving, Aaron Parviz had gone without notice. Suddenly, he leapt to his feet, with a crash of symbols. He swayed for a second, bringing his handgun to bear on Hafsah where she lay, unmoving.

I shot him three times, two in center mass and one through the head.

Horror and chaos had reigned supreme for less than ten seconds.

The room had gone totally silent again.

"Freeze, Federal Agents – Drop your weapons!" Someone yelled through a megaphone, his amplified voice booming in the smoke-filled silence.

We all froze in place. I wanted desperately to go to Hafsah, but I knew that if I moved, I would die.

Men in full combat gear with heavy weaponry, poured into the room from both front and back hallways.

We were quickly stripped of weapons and flung to the floor.

I landed next to Hafsah in a growing pool of her blood. Her beautiful brown eyes were closed and she didn't appear to be breathing.

I called her name as my arms were pinned behind my back and cable ties bit into my wrists. She didn't respond.

"Clear" Someone yelled.

A moment later I heard a voice I recognized.

"This is one hell of a mess, but I really like the location." I heard Jack say, with remarkably pure pitch and tone.

"This one's still alive." Someone said.

"Jack, its Hafsah. Help her, she's been shot." I pleaded.

"Medic!" He called.

A combat ready guy with a medical kit knelt beside Hafsah. He examined her quickly.

"We need to get her stabilized and transported, right now." He said.

From somewhere above and behind me, Jack called for an EMT from an ambulance that was evidently already outside.

He spoke to another agent standing over me.

"Take this guy and 'ginger girl' over there. Put them both in my vehicle. The other three go directly to Dallas." Jack directed.

Two guys hauled me to my feet and hustled me

into the back hallway where we passed a couple of ambulance gurneys being brought in by swiftly moving paramedics.

"We've got another live one." Someone called out from inside the studio.

"Hot diggity!" Jack said, with evident glee.

CHAPTER 47

As I was being shoved toward the rear exit of the recording studio, I looked back over my shoulder. Right behind me, Christine was being dragged along the hallway by another pair of heavily armored soldiers. I couldn't see her face because her head was down and her hair obscured my limited view.

The parking area behind the building was filled with big, black SUVs and emergency vehicles. Several firemen, federal agents and a couple of uniformed policemen watched as Christine and I were unceremoniously stuffed into the back seat of one of the SUVs. Our escorts left the doors open and stood watching us, with weapons ready.

Christine and I both had our hands bound behind us with cable ties cutting into our wrists. Christine laid her head back and I was able to see part of her face. Her red hair was plastered across it, but I could see the tears coursing down her cheeks. She let out a ragged sob.

My attention was drawn to a gurney being brought out the back of the building. Hafsah was strapped on it. She was quickly loaded into the back of an ambulance. Another SUV with red and blue lights flashing in the grill pulled ahead of the ambulance. The ambulance sirens bleated and the lights began flashing. The SUV followed by the ambulance, pulled away and disappeared from my view.

A moment later another gurney came out, with Jack right behind it. Jack watched as the ambulance was loaded and an escort vehicle pulled up. He turned toward us, as the two vehicles drove away.

Jack walked over and squatted on his heels just outside the open door where I was sitting.

"You're late, Jack." I said.

"Well, we had to stay out of sight until all the players showed up."

"How is she?"

"Do you mean your little friend from Mossad?"

"Tell me."

Just then, Anke, David, and Ben were brought out under heavy guard and immediately likewise stuffed individually into the back of three waiting black SUVs. Their grill lights flashing, the SUVs pulled away.

Jack caught my eye.

"Don't know about the woman. She's in pretty bad shape. Whatever happens, I'll make her disappear as if she had never existed. We've also got a wounded terrorist. If he lives, I'll have some fun with him. I have questions, and he will answer them."

"What about the other Mossad agents?"

"They'll be the subjects of a rendition. In about fifteen minutes, the three of them will be on a chopper headed for Dallas. From there an unmarked airplane will take them to one of our famous 'undisclosed locations'. We'll interrogate them and learn what we can. After that, they'll disappear, just like your lady friend. As I said, if she lives."

"They shut these guys down, Jack. They did your job for you. They deserve better treatment from our government."

"I'll decide what they deserve. If Israel wants any of them back, we might make some kind of deal. Now let's talk about you and your other lady friend here. Christine Valakova, Isn't it?"

Christine had composed herself and was now glaring at Jack. He ignored her and turned his attention back to me.

"Here's the thing. I have a file on you, my friend. It goes way back, like a hundred years back. This file hasn't been seen by very many people. I'll bet you'd like to keep it that way."

"What's your point?"

"I need you and Ms. Valakova to pretend none of this ever happened."

"Fine, not a problem."

"No, it's not as easy as all that. I know you, John. You're slippery. Let's be clear. I just made four Mossad agents disappear. I can do the same to you, your partner here, and her boyfriend – the cop. I'll make you all disappear. Got it? I know some folks who would love to get their hands on you, John. There are people in our government who believe you Shepherds really are ambassadors of heaven. We've been watching you for a long time. Certain people I know would like to take you apart so they can see what makes you tick. They think whatever strange genetic mutation you Shepherds have, could be the key to eternal life."

I could feel Christine trembling beside me.

"Now, John, I can either be your best friend or your worst enemy. It's up to you. If you piss me off, our records indicating you were actually born some time prior to 1911 under a different name could fall into the wrong hands. FBI Special Agent Doug Booker has taken a keen interest in you. He has some very powerful friends in Washington. I'd hate to see what might happen if he gained access to your file. Those people would like to know why you've been alive for so long with only minimal signs of aging. They'd want to ask you some questions related to certain events in world history. Then, they'll conduct a series of extensive and painfully invasive medical tests and experiments, followed by a meticulously thorough autopsy."

He paused to let me consider the implications of his threat. Then he shrugged.

"However, if you and I are still friends, I can keep those records sealed."

"That's cold, Jack. What did I ever do to you?"

He touched his jaw where I had hit him.

"You've made me uncomfortable. All that media attention to the, uh... shall we say – irregular FBI raid on a certain farmhouse, caused me a great deal of grief. I'm willing to forget you did that to me. I think the whole thing should just be forgotten. Don't you?"

"Forgotten, or forgiven?"

"Whatever, just so long as you keep your mouth shut. Can you do that?"

I hesitated. I wanted to make Jack sweat a little.

He pursed his lips.

"There's also the issue of your involvement in this matter. I can't have you talking about any of this, either." He made a vague but all-encompassing gesture with his hand. He looked me in the eye. "So, what's it gonna be?"

"OK, Jack. I promise you, neither myself, Christine, or Tony will say anything further about the FBI raid, or what happened here today. We'll act as though we have no knowledge of anything. Is that what you want?"

"I want you to swear to God."

I sighed in resignation.

"As God is my witness, I solemnly swear not to reveal any knowledge of any of the things we've just discussed, to anyone. I include Christine and Tony in this statement."

"There you go, buddy! That's what I'm talking about. I know you. You always adhere to any oath you swear. So, help you, God."

Jack turned to the nearest agent.

"Take these two to their office, and turn them loose. They're free to go. Then come straight back here."

"Yes sir." The agent said.

Jacked looked back at me and Christine

"Well, old buddy, I don't think we'll be seeing much of each other for a while. You folks have a nice day."

He turned and headed back toward the building.

As we were riding in the back of the big, black SUV with government plates, Christine turned to me and asked a question.

"What did you mean when you told that guy, he was late?"

I was stunned. After all she had just been through and what she had heard listening to the conversation with Jack. That was her question?

"His name is Jack McCarthy. He's a high ranking official with the Department of Homeland Security. I've known him a long time. He was assigned here to stop the local jihadists. I asked him to check out Hafsah and her story. From then on, I knew he would have us all under surveillance. He hacked our system and was privy to everything we said in our office, when we were all watching the news, planning the ambush, all of it. The whole time, I was feeding him things I wanted him to know. I knew he couldn't pass up any opportunity to stop the jihadists, or leave it entirely in our hands. He couldn't afford to take any chances. I was hoping he and his people would handle the whole thing. I thought they might jump Baha before he ever got to the studio. It didn't go down that way and now… Hafsah…" I choked. I couldn't say any more.

When we arrived at the high rise building which housed our office, the DHS agents cut the cable ties and turned us loose in the parking lot. Rubbing our wrists, we watched them drive away.

"Now what do we do?" Christine asked.

"Let's go up to the office. If you want to go home,

I'll call a cab. Once the hubbub dies down, we can probably pick up our vehicles at the studio, maybe later today. I imagine you'll want to call Tony. I don't know what will become of your purse and your cell phone or any of our personal effects we may have left in the studio. From now on, we can't talk about any of this. Someone will always be listening."

"John, are you alright? What's going to happen to Hafsah and the others?"

"No, Christine, I'm not alright. You heard what Jack said. The Mossad team will disappear. We'll never see any of them again. I'll never even know if Hafsah is alive or dead."

CHAPTER 48

On the elevator ride up to the third floor of our building, I looked over at Christine and said, "You've never asked any questions about the things Jack mentioned when he was threatening to expose me. Did you understand what he was saying?"

Christine looked back at me, and in her eyes I saw that confident look I had seen before.

"Of course, I understood what he was saying. I've always known you were different. You told me yourself, John. You're an ambassador of heaven."

"Do you understand what that means?"

Christine was thoughtful for a few heartbeats.

"It means you are a servant of the King. It means you have a mission here in this place, as a representative of the Kingdom of God. I don't understand everything about it, but I know it's true."

I nodded.

"Every child of the King has a responsibility to serve as an ambassador. We Shepherds are strangers in this place. This world is not our home. One day, I will get to go home, but until that day I must serve. The sheep need Shepherds."

The elevator doors opened onto our floor. We walked down the hall to the offices of Tucker Investigations. I typed in the access code to key the lock, letting us into the reception area. Intending to leave Christine at her desk, I was heading for my office. She stopped me with a statement.

"John, I have so many questions I don't even know where to begin."

Turning to look at her, I saw that although it wasn't even ten o'clock yet, she was nearly overwhelmed by the events of the morning. I had been so self-absorbed, I hadn't even noticed. Her makeup was smeared, her hair in disarray, and she had the shell-shocked look of someone who had just survived a gun fight. I realized she needed some comfort and reassurance.

"I'll tell you what I can, but don't you want to call Tony?"

"I can't, I mean… What do I tell him? He's up to his neck in alligators with the massacre at the mall. He was still on the scene when he called me about twelve hours ago. He only had a minute to tell me he was OK. We haven't spoken since. I tried to call him first thing this morning, but it went straight to voice mail. I can't tell him anything about…"

Tears began spilling down her face again.

I opened my arms and she nearly fell into my embrace. I held her.

For a moment, she cried quietly against my shoulder. Then, composing herself, she took a step back.

"OK. I'm going to the ladies' room. When I get back, you've got some 'splainin' to do." She tried to wink at me, but it lacked the spark of wit she intended.

While she was gone, I checked the phone messages. There was nothing out of the ordinary, business as usual. I knew going forward "as usual" was never going to be the same.

When Christine returned, she was fully put together. Other than the vague hints of strain around her eyes with their newly applied makeup, and a tension in her voice, she appeared fresh and ready to meet the demands of the day.

The two of us found seats in my office.

"Tell me what happens next," she said.

"I don't know what you mean."

"Well, if you're an ambassador of heaven, you must know what God is doing. You must know everything, about everything, right?"

I looked away, shaking my head.

"I wish it worked that way. I'm only a Shepherd. Our mission is to seek the lost, stand against the darkness and protect those entrusted to us. In the process we have some influence on the course of human events, but we have little knowledge of how our actions will do that until after the fact. My knowledge of the future is limited to what I learn as I go along. For much of my guidance I read the scriptures and pray — same as you."

"I don't get it. You act like an ordinary human? What does it mean to be a Shepherd?"

I looked in her eyes.

"I came to this planet in the same way you did, a child of human parents. I'm as human as you are."

"OK, so what's different about being a Shepherd?"

I shrugged.

"I was living the only life I knew. One day I realized how empty and shallow it was. I was given a glimpse of eternity. It was like a vision. I saw myself from the vantage point of God. It knocked me to my knees. I saw my sin and selfishness. Right then and there, I confessed my sin and repented. I asked God to forgive me and cleanse me. He did. In the process, I was changed.

I told Him I wanted to give Him my life. I felt a gentle tug, an invitation, and as I accepted it, He showed me what He would have me do. He showed me my heavenly home, the time line of eternity, and the plan from the beginning. I saw the patriarchs of old, and met the first Shepherd, the Great Shepherd, His own son, who asked me to serve in this place. He showed me what it would cost me, and how I would be equipped for service. I accepted the call."

"If God is omnipresent and omnipotent as I believe He is, why does He need servants? I mean, He could make everyone and everything become exactly the way He wants."

"He doesn't need anything, but His ways are not our ways, Christine. Sure, He could make us all behave like perfect puppets. We could have a perfect world. When I had that vision, I had a limited sense of His incredible Majesty. It was so overwhelming, words cannot express it. I saw as though through a filtered lens, a glimpse of His intent. All of creation, everything we can observe about Cosmos, Chronos, even Kairos, are but an infinitesimally small fraction of His works. What we call the universe is limited in our understanding, and it's only a dust particle in a distant corner of His creation. He has set in motion and given structure to the tiniest individual thing, and the most complex and immense systems. There are dimensions and aspects of His creation we can't see or even begin to imagine. As a part of all of that, He made us. In all of creation we were the only thing He made in His image. We're the only living thing, with the capacity to be a little bit like Him. One of the aspects of being a little like Him means being able to imagine, create, and choose our destiny."

"As wonderful as all that sounds, it doesn't answer my question." Christine said.

"He made us and He loves us. Our relationship with Him is different from that of any other created being. Like the angels, we can choose to honor him and be obedient, or not. He made us as spiritual beings in temporary physical bodies, living on a planet with a limited shelf life. If we choose to, we can live with Him in paradise forever. If we choose not to, we will live separate from Him forever, in continual torment.

Seeing this, the angel Lucifer determined to thwart the desire of God and set himself in the place of God. It was Lucifer's plan to make humans subservient to him that caused sin and death to enter creation. Once humans chose to listen to the devil and stopped believing what God had told them, they and all creation in this small part of the galaxy were doomed under the law of sin and death. Everything is created by God, even sin and death. Just as there are laws governing physics and mathematics, there are laws governing life and death, good and evil, and what we call infinity and eternity. He made those as well. God has always known what would happen, because he created all things and knows everything about his created things. He knew about the fall and the consequences. He had already prepared a way for the lost to be redeemed. This is something even the angels don't understand."

"What does any of that have to do with Shepherds?"

"The devil has legions of fallen angels tasked to mislead, corrupt, and ultimately doom the sheep. God chose certain people to become Shepherds among the sheep, so there would always be someone who stood against the darkness and protected those sheep destined to come back to the Creator. We help maintain the order of events. He could have done it some other way, but this is the way He chose. He placed Shepherds to guard His sheep."

Christine nodded, and flashed a smile.

"His sheep am I" she said.

"I know."

"You said something before about the cost of being a Shepherd. What's that about?"

"Shepherds are blessed with long lives compared to other people. I only age about one year for every ten years you do. Consequently, I've watched generations of people die.

If I were to marry and have a family, I would watch all of them grow old and die, while I barley aged at all. Everyone — everyone, I've ever loved or ever will, all my friends and family, have been or will be taken from me by death. The life of a Shepherd is one of continual loss.

She thought about that for a moment.

"What would that mean for you and Hafsah?"

I rubbed my face with my hands.

"I don't know. I've been struggling with that. Maybe God took her from me, to spare me the agony of outliving her. Maybe I made a mistake getting involved with her in the first place. I thought maybe God was giving me some sort of gift, but... Christine... I just don't know."

CHAPTER 49

When I walked out of the building, I was surprised to see my homeless friend Dustin, leaning on his shopping cart, just outside the entrance. He grinned when he saw me.

"Hello, Good Angel. How you be?" He said.

"It's been a terrible morning, Dustin. I don't feel like talking right now."

"Yo heart is heavy. Um hum. You feelin' let down."

"Something like that. Say, aren't you sort of far from your usual stomping grounds?"

He pointed at me.

"Not far. 'Sides, this where you at."

"Me. Were you looking for me? How did you know where to find me?"

Dustin smiled and pointed at the sky. "A little birdie told me."

"OK. What can I do for you?"

"I ain't here for that."

Sometimes Dustin's ramblings annoy me. He seldom gets straight to the point.

"OK. What's up?"

"Right, right. He's restorin' yo sight. Yo eyes been in darkness. Do you see the light?"

This was the last thing I needed right then, more of his enigmatic messages. I gritted my teeth and tried to be polite.

"Dustin, I'm in no mood for this. I've got a rental car coming."

"Uh uh. What's comin' ain't no rental. Ain't the car yo expectin', neither."

"What are you talking about?"

"Abide. You gots to abide. Don't you be runnin'. Don't step aside."

I took a deep breath. I nearly sobbed in the process.

"That's right, Good Angel. Let it go, all that resentment, poisonin' yo soul."

I was speechless. How did he know?

"What are you saying?" I asked.

"Faith, hope and love. Is you missin' something? You think you lost something. Maybe you lost the wrong thing."

"I don't understand."

"Faith, hope and love. You gots to have um all. You lose even one, you gonna fall."

As usual, he was looking around vaguely as though he was trying to spot something in the distance, but wasn't sure where to look.

"What do you know about loss?" I asked.

"More'n most. You see how I is."

I did. Dustin was brain damaged from injuries he had sustained in battle. Homeless, in a land of wealth. Alone, in a community of over a hundred thousand people. Yet, he held on to his faith, hope and love.

"You be thinkin' you can't stand to lose what you don't even have. You don't have, 'cause you don't ask. You don't ask, 'cause you missin' something. Faith, hope and love. What you missin'?" He asked.

That was a good question. What was missing in my life? Which of the three? If one was missing, how did I change that?

I nodded.

"Yeah, I think I catch your drift."

"That's it then. All I know. I gots me my rounds. I gots to go."

"Hold on a minute, Dustin. You said something was coming. What is it?"

Dustin grinned from ear to ear.

"Hee, hee, hee. Can't say. Gots to go. 'N if I told you, then you'd know." He winked at me and started pushing his shopping cart across the parking lot. As he walked away, I think he was whistling "Stairway to Heaven."

I was standing there in the parking lot, watching him walk away, when a car pulled up beside me.

"Are you Mr. Tucker?" The driver asked, through the open window.

"Yes, I'm John Wesley Tucker."

He turned off the engine, grabbed some paperwork, and stepped out of the vehicle.

"OK, sir. This is your rental. If you'll sign here, I'll give you the keys."

As I signed the paperwork, the rental agent told me I was good to go. A car was coming to pick him up once I took possession of the vehicle. As soon as the keys were in my hand, I jumped in and drove in search of Dustin. Evidently, he had taken one of the paved trails into Rose Rudman Park. There was no convenient place to park at this entrance except the parking lot I had just pulled out of, so I had to let him go.

As usual, for all his ramblings and the strange way he recounted his message, he made more sense than all the talking heads on television and radio. I smiled to myself. To think he called me, "Good Angel".

CHAPTER 50

The massacre at the shopping mall in Tyler was still the top story on all the news channels. There was much discussion about the armed citizens who returned fire in the shooting melee. Was it a good thing or a bad thing? In other news, a brief story on the local channel began with an announcement from The Texas Rangers. They were holding a man named Kevin Watkins on a suspicion of murder charge. The interesting part being his claim he was the only survivor of the FBI raid on the white supremacists meeting connected with the murder of the Gregg County District Attorney, some weeks previously. He said he witnessed a drone strike on the farm house where the group was meeting. His story created a little buzz, for about five minutes. There was no mention of my part in his capture.

The President of the United States appeared on television to speak about the atrocities perpetrated by religious fundamentalists on the people of Tyler, Texas. He announced that all of the terrorists were killed by federal agents during a raid on their training camp. Tragically, a game warden was killed on the scene. He applauded the wonderful and swift work of the FBI and the Department of Homeland Security, in bringing the religious radicals to justice.

After that, the focus was on the individual victims of the outrageous attack in the shopping mall. I made a point of attending every memorial service I could. I was just another face in the crowds, just another face, with tears streaming down my cheeks. Sorrowful for the pain of those grieving their losses.

An interesting wrinkle in the story of the jihadi massacre was a few of the victims were at the Kyle Coltrane concert the night before the attack. The whole concert was being filmed and recorded for use on a "live" album and a documentary. Bootlegged video footage of Nat Baha and the Honky Tonk Broncs performance appeared on social media and went viral. His music was even being played on the radio.

While we were all still reeling from the recent horror. Within a week, it happened again. Home grown terrorists made a machine gun attack on a shopping mall in Medford, Oregon. While the shock of that was hitting, there was a bombing of a theater in Albuquerque, New Mexico. Two days later, jihadist gunmen shot up the people in the stands at a high school football game in Dubuque, Iowa, and there was an attack at a festival in Bangor, Maine. Within two weeks, four other cities in four other states were likewise attacked in the name of Allah. The same things were happening in Europe and across the globe. The whole world was being terrorized in the cause of Islamic jihad.

In many countries, martial law became the rule and people were being deprived of the freedoms they had previously enjoyed. Angry citizens took up arms against their innocent Muslim neighbors, committing horrible crimes. There wasn't anywhere in the world where peace was assured. Nowhere anyone could feel safe. Every country with a strong infrastructure and relative economic health struggled to maintain at least a façade of life as usual.

Then, a magnitude 8.6 earthquake in central California took over the news cycles, with images of fire, destruction and death. The devastation was cataclysmic. Hundreds of thousands of people were killed, millions were homeless. Emergency services were hampered. All the highways were impassable and the airports were unusable. The only way to deliver supplies or rescue people was by helicopter or by sea. The navy played a vital part in preventing further loss of life. It seemed like the entire world was involved in the relief effort.

As the first days of fall drifted by like wind-blown leaves, life continued in a sad and sickly semblance of former normalcy. Daily, we were informed of new humanitarian crisis caused by catastrophic storms and military conflicts in diverse places.

In the ongoing battle against Islamic extremism in the Middle East, the city of Damascus, Syria was completely destroyed. There was speculation the Russians were providing Iran with material support, speeding the development of nuclear weapons.

The Islamic Caliphate announced, after centuries of waiting — the Ummah unanimously confirmed the true Mahdi. The Mahdi was the promised one — the man who would bring peace and unite the world for Islam

Christine and I did our best to meet our client's needs, even as aspects of the wider world were plunging into greater chaos.

I came whistling into the office on a Monday morning and approached Christine sitting at her desk. She was staring at her computer monitor.

"John, have you seen this?"

"Seen what?"

"Our bank statement, it's showing a deposit of two hundred and fifty thousand dollars. Do you know anything about it?"

"Hmmm, maybe a little. I suspect our client in Israel applied it as a payment for services rendered in the Nat Baha case. You should contact the bank to determine there hasn't been some mistake. Just to be certain."

"Ok, I hope you're right. You seem to be in a rather good mood this morning, what's up?"

I smiled at her and handed her a plain white envelope addressed to me, with no return address.

"On Friday evening, I found this in my mailbox along with the usual pile of advertising. Snail mail, we tend to forget about it because it's slow, pretty low tech and under the radar. As you can see, the postmark over the stamp is from Los Angeles."

Christine took the letter out of the envelope and began to read.

"Dear, mystery man, (or should I call you, Earl?)

I thought I'd take a moment to drop you a line. Our mutual friend has completely recovered from her medical condition and is in good health. I'm sorry to say, although her physical health is good, her emotional state is not. She is suffering great sorrow at the loss of a loved one. It seems the man in her life is missing.

All of us have returned home and are fully engaged in our former activities. I've been instructed to thank you for your fine work and assistance with our crisis situation of a few weeks ago. I believe you'll find the payment to be sufficient to compensate for your efforts and any additional expense you may have incurred. Please say a warm Texas "Howdy" to Christine for us.

Oh, by the way. Our mutual friend is going to be performing in a concert with the London Symphony Orchestra, in Paris, on the 23rd of this month. You should check it out.

All my love, until we meet again,

Anke

Christine looked up with tears in her eyes.

"Oh, John…"

It was all she could say.

I grinned at her.

"Would you do me a favor? I have to make some phone calls and handle a few business details. I'll be tied up for about an hour. I don't want to be disturbed until I've finished. Would you be kind enough to make arrangements for transportation to, and accommodation in, Paris? I'm going to a concert."

Christine smiled, blinking away tears.

"Yes, of course. What departure and return arrangements would you like?"

I chewed on it for a moment. I had all weekend to think about it.

"One way to Paris, departure tomorrow the 21st. We'll leave the return open."

Christine nodded. She was grinning now.

I handed her my passport.

"One other thing — book everything in the name on this passport. Don't worry. You're not breaking any laws. At least none that matter"

Christine studied the passport and looked up at me with wide eyes.

"Thanks, Christine. When I've finished my business here, I'll be going out. As I'm leaving the office, I'll check with you on the itinerary."

CHAPTER 51

I had been working at my desk for about an hour and twenty minutes. I took a moment to look around at my beautifully appointed office. I admired my heavily carved oak desk and the two upholstered chairs in front of it. I stood and walked over to a window and looked out over the city. I always found peace as I surveyed the park like topography. I was reminded again of how blessed I was to have met Christine when I did. By divine appointment, she was the one who had found this office space and done such a gracious job of furnishing it. Everything was as it was meant to be.

As I was leaving to run some errands, I stopped by her desk.

"Ok, John, at 8:00 AM, tomorrow, I have you flying out of Tyler Pounds to Dallas DFW. You connect in DFW for a 10.05 flight to Paris PAR, with a one hour and twenty-five-minute layover at JFK. That might be a tight connection. I have you arriving in Paris at 5:50 AM, on the 22nd. How does that sound?"

"Perfect. Where will I be staying when I get there?"

"I have you booked into the Pavillon de la Reine on the Place des Vosges. It's only a four-star hotel, but this was rather short notice. Oh, there's a shuttle from the airport, and you can ride the metro to the

Parc de la Villette."

"What's that?"

"It's where the concert will be. In the Grande Salle-Pierre Boulez, in the Philharmonie de Paris. It's the newest, most modern and acoustically brilliant concert hall in Europe. Wait till you see it! From a distance it looks like a giant spaceship sitting on the ground. Your ticket will be waiting for you at the hotel."

"Well done, Christine. I'm impressed."

"Nothing to it. Glad I could help."

"Listen, I have some errands to run. I won't be back till later this afternoon. We'll need to talk. Will you be here?"

Christine looked concerned.

"Of course, what's up?"

"I'll explain it all when I get back."

I returned to the office at about three fifteen to find Christine on the telephone with a client. I left my door open so she would know to come into my office when she finished the phone call. She walked in a few minutes later looking concerned.

"So, is there a problem?" I asked her.

"You tell me. You're the mystery man." She said, sitting down in front of my desk.

"No, I meant with the client."

"It's just business as usual. What did you want to talk about?"

I've always appreciated people who get right to the point.

"I've been thinking…"

Christine rolled her eyes.

"Oh boy, here we go!" She said.

I chuckled. How many conversations had we had like this? I had a special knack for making Christine roll her eyes.

"Here's the deal. As you know, I'm going to be out of the country for a while. I don't know for how long, or what's going to happen. You're going to manage all aspects of the business while I'm away. I've transferred the ownership of the agency to you..."

"What? No, John, I don't want you to do that!"

I held my hand up to stop her outburst.

"It's already done. You'll need to sign some paperwork with our attorney tomorrow, but it's a done deal. Consider it a wedding gift."

"No. What are you thinking? Are you even planning to come back?"

"I don't know, and that's the point. Christine, you've learned everything you need to know to manage this agency. In fact, you've been instrumental in making it what it is today. I'd appreciate it if you would continue the name, 'Tucker Investigations', but other than that, it's all yours to run anyway you want to. I should point out, there's a certain Detective Lieutenant of the Tyler PD, approaching twenty years on the force. Tony might be willing to retire from public service and go into private practice. I can't imagine a better team of investigators."

Christine was silent. Her eyes filled with tears, threatening to spill down her cheeks.

I pretended to ignore her subdued display of emotion.

"Oh, I almost forgot. I've arranged to give up my apartment. I'd appreciate it if you would dispose of my furniture and whatever else I leave behind, which includes my truck. Actually, the truck belongs to the agency, so you may want to keep it. It's mighty useful to have."

I set the keys on my desk. Christine snatched the box of tissues instead, and began to dab at her eyes, blotting away the tears.

"I'll leave the truck here and take a taxi to my apartment and to the airport in the morning." I mumbled.

"Like hell, you will!" She snapped. "I'll drive you to your apartment, and Tony and I will take you to the airport in the morning."

I started to say something, but she wasn't having it.

"Shut up! I don't want to hear another word. You listen to me. You have some firearms and other equipment the agency wants to buy. I don't intend to leave them in your apartment. Let's go take care of that, right now."

Christine stood up and spun toward the door, leaving the truck keys on the desktop as she marched away. I'm no expert on women's behavior, but I figured she was trying to tell me the conversation was over.

Twenty-four hours after Christine and I left the office, I was flying over the Atlantic Ocean at 38,000 feet, semi-reclined in a first-class seat on an Air France jet. I was looking at my tablet, reading the news. As usual, the news was mostly horrible, and entirely predictable.

It seemed there was an increased level of sun spot activity. Solar flares were becoming more pronounced. Many speculated this could accelerate global climate change, with unpredictable consequences. Others were concerned one or more electromagnetic pulses might well disrupt communications or damage significant portions of the electrical grid, possibly affecting the entire planet.

In a related story, we were told the reason the moon was continually blood red, to all observers, was due to an unforeseen cloud of cosmic dust particles passing between the earth and the moon. That same dust cloud, coupled with the massive ash cloud created by the volcanos recently erupting in Greenland, Japan, and Chile, was also blamed for obscuring large areas of the night sky. It now appeared as if millions of the stars and even familiar constellations had simply disappeared. There was speculation there might also be something in the volcanic ash causing the death of millions of birds worldwide, as well as the massive fish kills in all of the world's oceans.

In Russia, an unprecedented earth quake destroyed most of the city of Moscow, causing another humanitarian crisis and disrupting the flow of natural gas and oil into and out of the region. The quake and aftershocks had been felt all the way to China in the east, Portugal in the west, Turkey in the south and Artic regions to the north. There was considerable damage done throughout the Balkan's.

The latest outbreak of a new strain of Ebola in West Africa now claimed nearly twenty-five thousand lives and an estimated one hundred thousand were sickened. United Nations troops were dispatched to aid in controlling the widespread panic and resulting violence. Containment was failing. It was believed hundreds, if not thousands of people (an unknown number infected) might have fled the region, possibly traveling to Europe and the United States. The World Health Organization feared the epidemic would spread beyond the African continent and become a worldwide pandemic. We were told there was no need for concern because the standard of medicine in developed countries was lightyears ahead of that in the third world. Even if Ebola spread across the globe, the death toll might be reasonably small.

In other news, the Mahdi announced he was calling on all Islamic fighters throughout the world to cease hostilities against the infidels. He believed it was time for a cessation of violence and a season of peace. Further, he declared he was in support of allowing the building of the Hebrew Temple in Jerusalem! He himself would leave Medina to take up residence in Damascus, where he would oversee the rebuilding of the war-torn city.

I thought about what the Mahdi said. It would take some time, but within three and half years or so, he might just be able to get it done. The Mahdi might be able to calm the raging madness and bring peace to the world. For a time. After all, it would fit the plan.

I looked around the passenger cabin, half expecting to hear a trumpet call and see seats being vacated, but somehow sensing, while the hour was much nearer, the clock was still ticking. The time was not yet at hand.

A pretty female flight attendant in a fitted gray skirt with a starched white blouse and a red, white, and blue neck scarf saw me looking around. She approached and asked with a smile,

"Je peux vous apporter une autre tasse de café, Monsieur Shepherd?"

I smiled back.

Yes, another cup of coffee would be nice. After all, sometimes coffee fuels my mission.

****

The End

Is not yet here.

EPILOGUE

Most people lead lives of solitary anxiety. Solitary, because they don't talk about their fears with anyone. They don't even want to admit they have them.

They don't know who they are, or why they are on the earth.

Introspection only brings more doubts and fears, so they seek solace from science.

Science tells them they are just carbon-based biological organisms, evolved from the muck, eking out a brief existence at the expense of a doomed planet. Science tells them life is random, meaningless and pointless. Take another pill, and try not to think about it.

The clock is ticking.

Many are wandering through life, aimlessly waiting for the clock to run out. Some are seeking something to make them feel as if their life matters in some way. They mostly want to "do the right thing", but violently disagree on what "right" is, because, "Every way of a man is right, in his own eyes."

The clock is ticking.

People know, from the moment of birth, they are doomed. They know life is short and uncertain. It may end at any time. The best of them ask, "why"?

Why do we exist? Why are we the way we are? Why do bad things happen? Why is there suffering and death? What happens after we die? Do we just cease to exist? When we die, will it be as if we had never existed at all?

The world offers many different and conflicting answers. Most of them are lies.

So, most people everywhere, in every walk of life, are as lost as sheep without a shepherd, stumbling blindly through however many days remain to them, silently screaming in desperation.

The clock is ticking.

I know why I get up in the morning. I know what I'm supposed to do, and how I should do it. I live to serve, but I don't serve the planet earth, a government, or myself.

I serve the holy God; the creator of all things. I am appointed as one of His ambassadors in this place.

I serve The Good Shepherd.

He alone is perfect.

Like me, His sheep are imperfect, but His sheep know His voice when they hear it.

Other sheep wander around lost; following whatever voices sound most pleasant to them at the moment, even the voices leading them to slaughter.

The wolves prowl among them, picking sheep off one at a time, sometimes whole flocks, en masse.

Sheep without a shepherd are helpless against the predators.

I am appointed as a Shepherd of His sheep, to seek the lost sheep, and stand against the wolves.

We who serve as Shepherds are imperfect, but we are empowered and equipped for service.

I have the sword of Truth, the message of glorious hope.
I have work to do.
I wish I were a better Shepherd.
The clock is ticking.

****

If you liked this take a look at:

Murder at Cluster Springs Raceway
by John Theo Jr.

A deadly auto accident at a southern Virginia racetrack draws private investigator Brandon Hall into a new case. When young race car driver Drew Schilling dies in a fiery crash, his politician father hires Brandon to investigate. Virginia Senator Gregory Schilling believes his son's death was not an accident, but a politically motivated murder.

With the help of friends, Brandon uncovers evidence which ties the raceway death to the rapidly changing political landscape in the United States. Radicalized groups, promoting violence on college campuses and cities, have found their way into rural southern Virginia. Enter the corrupt world of Washington DC politics, old Dixieland families, and the volatile culture wars unfolding within the United States.

Murder at Cluster Springs Raceway is a tale straight from Virginia, and national, headlines.

Available now on Amazon

ABOUT THE AUTHOR

Born in Bakersfield, California and abandoned by his parents in Seattle, Washington. After living in the foster care system for some years, Dan Arnold was eventually adopted. He's traveled internationally, lived in Idaho, Washington, California, Virginia, and now makes his home in Texas with his wife Lora. They have four grown children and three grandchildren of whom they are justifiably proud, not because they are such good parents, but because God is good.

A Member of the Association of Christian Fiction Writers, and Western Writers of America, in 2015, writing under the name Daniel Roland Banks, his book Angels & Imperfections was selected as a finalist in Christian Fiction in the Reader's Favorite International Book awards.

Find more great titles by Dan Arnold and Christian Kindle News at https://christiankindlenews. com/our-authors/dan-arnold/